I0744384

Published by: Cinnabar Moth Publishing LLC
Santa Fe, New Mexico

Cover Design by: Ira Geneve

ISBN-13: 978-1-953971-85-2
Library of Congress Control Number: 2023936608

Izzy Hoffman is Not a Witch

ALYSSA ALESSI

Prologue

Every morning I wake from the same dream. Honestly, it's more like a nightmare. I walk up to a ridiculously large brass-framed mirror, its dirty gold trim holding golden vines wrapped around its curves. Faces belonging to chubby baby angels are carved in its crevices. I'm hesitant to look at first, but then I jump in front of it like I know what's coming and want to get it over with. I do know what's coming. My reflection is the same every time. A woman with long straggly black hair and a gaunt face stares back at me. She has no eyes, yet she looks straight into my soul. Her head moves from side to side. My chest aches with each crook of her neck. She wants to pull me in, I know she does. Her bony fingers scratch at the sides of the glass. I open my mouth to scream, but the shriek comes from her unhinged jaw instead of mine. I always wake in a puddle of sweat, then get up to brush my teeth. This has been on repeat for five years, until today. Today is my twelfth birthday and as a gift, this woman smiled and punched through the glass.

Chapter 1

As the glass shatters, my eyes pop open. My bedroom door swings forward so hard it bounces off the door stop.

"Happy birthday to ya! Happy birthday to ya!" The birthday parade around my room is in full effect. I smile, because even though I'm too old for this, my parents look hilarious.

"Thanks guys," I giggle while I sit up to hug my mom.

"You're looking a little sweaty honey; do you want me to open up a window in here?" My dad kisses my cheek, his coarse beard stubble scratching my skin. He opens a window to let the cool October breeze rush in. I'm not sweating because I'm hot, I'm sweating because Bony Witch broke through the glass and changed the dream that has been the same for as long as I can remember. I will never admit to my parents that I'm still having these dreams, or the fact I named *her*. I used to cry out at night, but checking the closets and turning on lights became useless.

"Izzy? Are you ok?" mom asks. A navy-blue wizard hat stands tall on her head, and a black boa drapes snake like around her neck. Her outfit says *silly*, but her face says *I'm worried about my strange child.* I hate when my mom looks at me like that. Her left eyebrow all raised and her big brown eyes burning holes in my skin. It's like she has some sort of mom superpower that detects when I'm even just a little uncomfortable.

"What? Yeah, I'm fine," I lie. "Maybe… I'm getting a little old for the birthday parade, you know?" I search their faces for any hint of them not believing me.

My parents exchange a look. I feel bad once I say it out loud, but it was that or bring up my dream.

"Pfft, you are never too old for a birthday parade, but we can tone it down a bit next year if you'd like," my mom compromises.

"Speak for yourself Loretta! I'm still wearing my cloak next year!" dad jokes, while swinging the cape in front of his face like a vampire would. He opens his mouth wide every time he laughs, showing off his perfect bright teeth against his smooth dark skin.

"I'm not too old for the pancakes, though," I laugh giving them a sly smirk.

"Mm Hmm…" my mom smiles and gets up from my bed, tossing all the fluffy blankets behind her.

Dad looks out the window at the growing crowd and says, "Alright birthday girl, we have a shop to open so let's get them pancakes before it gets too late," in a tone too serious for his outfit.

To my dad it's just a shop, but to my mom and I, it's home. My dad always teases "you girls should just set up sleeping bags down there and I'll see you in the morning!" Dark Alley Books has been our family bookshop for generations. From the outside, it's a large brick building with glass windows showcasing jack-o-lanterns and string lights year-round. Like most buildings on our side street, it holds a shop on the bottom level and a home on the second. Next to our olive-green door there is a plaque that reads "J YOUNG 1641". J Young is my ancestor from my mom's side. All I know is he built this building, and for almost four hundred years, my family has sold books out of it. We don't just sell books anymore, we also sell t-shirts that say "Witch City" with a silhouette of a witch flying on a broom across the chest. Mugs, hats, socks, and other boring things that have nothing to do with books also sit on our shelves. It isn't just Dark Alley Books that sells these. The corner store, literally named The Cornah Store, sells the same crap. The hardware store, the pharmacy—everywhere you turn you'll see the witch logo. We sell things for the tourists. Every October our little town of Marblehead (aka nowhere even remotely cool, New England) gets flooded with tourists.

Since today is October first, there will be a line down the block for every store on our downtown street. It's like this is the only area tourists bother to check out. Do they not know about the arcade on the other side of town? Or the view from the cliff at Dead Horse Beach? They don't care, they just want souvenirs with a picture of a witch on it, to show everyone they came here. To show they visited the famous "witch city." The town that celebrates Halloween like no other.

My predictions were correct. I step onto the cobblestone and immediately a woman in an elaborate witch costume yells "Hey kid! You open?"

"No." I scoff with zero enthusiasm.

My parents love the customers because "They are what's keeping us alive Izzy! Without them we'd just have a family library!" And? I'd be good with that. The corner in the back could be for just me. The nook in the back of the shop is my sanctuary, and I don't like when customers touch my stuff. There is a table set up with dozens of bowls filled with all different types of crystals. Each one is unique, varying in color, size, and texture. And they are supposed to have healing powers. We sell books on crystals, so I know that Rose Quarts is for love, Tourmaline is for protection, and Amethyst for healing... supposedly. I don't believe any of it, but I still love touching them all. I feel like when everyone else comes in and touches them, it ruins how they feel for me. It's stupid, but they are mine.

I'm thinking about my crystals and watching my reflection in the windows as I walk by each store. I love watching my waist-length hair blow behind me as I walk and catching when my lip gloss shines in the sun against my mocha complexion. There is something about storefront window reflections that make you look way cooler than you do in real life. I can hear my mom's voice in my head, "You're daydreaming again Izzy…" and smash! I collide with a man and fall to the ground. I hit my head so hard on the brick that I must be asleep because Bony Witch is all I see. She paces back and forth in the mirror. The concerned look on her face sending a hint of fear to my gut. She is biting her claw-like nails and grabbing her own face. Suddenly she stops. She catches me watching her and dashes full speed towards the mirror.

I wake up on the ground to an elderly woman with her hand out to help me up.

"Sweetie, are you hurt? That man just knocked you down and kept going! People these days, rude as ever, I tell you!"

"Yeah, thanks" I say a bit confused. My head is killing me, and the slight dizziness is throwing me off. I see the man who I collided with and feel a chill crawl from my fingertips up my arms. He is tall and thin, with his calf-length black leather coat blowing behind him as he tries to flee the scene. The old lady is still going on about how back in her day gentlemen did the right thing, but I'm focused on catching up with that guy. I'm not sure what I'm going to say when I do but I want to get a better look at least.

"I know, right? So rude! Thanks again!" I yell to the lady as I start to run. He turns the corner on Derby St. but by the time I get there the street is completely crowded, and he's gone. I lost him.

Chapter 2

The bell above the door rings as I step into "Witches Brew", my best friend's coffee shop. The place is packed, and I hear "double espresso mocha! Iced vanilla chai! Small black Americano!" Orders are being yelled out to all the nameless customers. Usually you hear, "Joe, Carmella!" and other actual names because Nat's mom knows all her regulars' names.

"Izzy!" Nat swings her arms around me as if she hasn't seen me in weeks. "Happy birthday bestie! Omg those boots are so hot!" she says, giving my birthday outfit the influencer approval.

Nat is seriously the best. Her smile makes everyone smile, and she always has tons of energy. She says she drinks decaf lattes but I'm not sure. She's a lot shorter than I am, even though her bouncy curls give her at least an extra three inches. Her eyes are a light amber color, and really pop against her brown freckled skin. She's probably the most gorgeous girl in our grade, but more importantly, she's the most fun.

"Come to the back, I have a surprise for you!" She drags me by the arm to our favorite booth, furthest from the register but still a seat at the window.

"I hope it's a new sweater because you stretched the heck out of this one," I complain while holding up the arm that she practically ripped off in excitement. We plop down in the eggplant-purple cushions across from one another as she waves her hand at me to say *open it already*! I slowly unwrap the glittery paper to find a beautifully bold crystal necklace. It looks like five of my black crystals all pushed together to make one. A perfect black prism held by a delicate piece of silver and a thick black string.

"Nat! You totally get me. Thanks, this is gorgeous!" I mean it, it's the perfect gift. It is so long that I don't need to unclasp it to put it on. I flip my hair out from under it and give Nat my best smile. "How do I look?"

She whips out her phone and yells, "like this post will get a million likes!" She snaps a selfie of us and says she's going to post a birthday shout out to me online. "It's black obsidian, by the way. I got it from a witch. She said it will help protect you from negative energy."

"A witch? You mean the creepy lady from the tarot shop?"

"Yes, and Miss Clara knows what she's talking about. She said she thinks you're a witch too, you know."

I laugh so hard that I spit my water out on the table. "I like crystals so I'm a witch? You have a black cat, does that make you a witch too? Don't believe anything anyone says this month. People just want to put on a good show for the tourists."

Nat laughs and says, "Uh yeah, have you seen our sandwich specials? My mom changed our avocado toast to monster mash!" We both shake our heads at the desperate attempt to please these Halloween-obsessed visitors.

Nat and I gather our things to take the walk down to the beach like we've planned for days. The beach is our escape from the madness. As we pass the witch statue in town square, people are gathering to take pictures with it. The witch is a fictional witch from a TV show from the nineties. A bronze, teenaged witch with a bookbag and a black cat is the attraction of town square. I bet they don't even read the plaque. If they did, they would learn that this was the site where women were hung for witchcraft. In their defense, the plaque is very small. I don't think people want to remember such sad things. It's much easier to focus on the fun of the statue and how good your Halloween costume looks while you are posing next to her. You know, ignore the bad stuff but hashtag Witch City.

"Ew, old people selfies," Nat whispers.

I don't laugh, because I'm thinking about the morbid fact that they are standing where someone died.

When we get to the cliff overlooking the beach, it's even more beautiful than it was two weeks ago. Things change so fast this time of year. It's like the sun knows it has to shine brighter to keep us warm or something. The light sparkles off the near-freezing ocean as the waves crash against the rocky gray sand. Hundreds of little boats sit docked because their owners are stuck at work. The maple trees that line the cliff are already a flaming red. Nat takes a sip of her latte and has that look on her face.

"What?" I ask suspiciously.

"Oh, come on, let me take a picture of you! I won't post it. It will just be for us. Your all-black aesthetic against these red trees is so vogue."

I do want to show off the new platform Doc Martens that my parents gave me this morning.

"Ok, whatever. But promise, no posting."

Nat is so obsessed with taking pictures. I like taking pictures too, but they never look good enough to post in my opinion.

"Pinky promise," she agrees.

I clasp my hands together and lift my left leg to make sure my boots are in the photo. "So hot!" Nat yells out. We sit under a tree with our backs resting against a craggy oak. Nat's face goes blank.

"Hey, what's up? Not enough likes on your last post?" I ask, teasing just a bit. She holds her phone up to show me the picture. A shadow hovers over me in a nearby willow tree and I know right away it is Bony Witch. I feel a chill run down my spine and the sour taste of vomit in the back of my throat. Never in my life has a shadow appeared in one of my photos. I scan the trees and nearby benches, but not a soul in sight. No boys from school, hiding childishly behind a bush laughing and pointing. No weird lights making shadows, it's *her*.

"This looks like a ghost! And it looks totally real Izzy. I'm not messing with you, I swear."

I stare at the monster from my dreams. "She's coming for me." The words come out so soft that Nat asks me to repeat. "She's coming for me!" I scream. My voice cracks in frustration.

"Who?" Nat's normally perky face is pale with worry. She seems scared, not watching a scary movie scared, but scared like you turned the movie off and now you have to walk to the bathroom by yourself scared. Imagine if she saw this woman as often as I did.

"Never mind. I need to get to the shop," I say beginning to stomp away. I avoided bringing *her* up this morning and I'd like to avoid it again.

"Izzy, stop! What is this, you're creeping me out. You can talk to me. Besties for life, remember?" Her hand on my arm and the look in her eyes tell me she is sincere.

I deep sigh because she's right. "Remember the dreams I had as a kid? The lady in the mirror?" I keep my eyes closed while talking, to hide the embarrassment.

"When we like eight years old? Yeah, I guess."

I'm already regretting telling her, but I've already started. "I never stopped dreaming about her. And last night she broke through the glass. I feel weird, like really weird. I bumped into this guy earlier and she flashed in my head again. I tried to follow him, but lost him on Derby, and now this. I don't know what to do."

Nat is looking at me like she probably wouldn't believe me if it weren't for the picture she just took. "You know what? Miss Clara is such a fraud. She said this necklace would protect you. She lied! There wouldn't be some shadow hag bothering you if this was real," she says shaking her head slowly.

Why the heck would Miss Clara think I need protection? Maybe she isn't as full of crap as I thought. Note to self: visit Miss Clara.

Chapter 3

My mom makes the best birthday cake. "An old family recipe," she winks whenever I tell her that. I'm sitting in the graphic-novel section of our bookshop eating my third slice when I hear my mom talking to a customer. She is usually upbeat with anyone who walks through the door, and even more so during the busy season, but she sounds awkward at best right now. Her voice is trembling a bit, and she sounds like she is trying to be stern.

"Sir, you are going to have to leave. I'm sorry I can't help you."

I shove the strawberry bit from the top of my cake in my mouth and get up to get a peek at what's going on. I poke my head from around the corner and stop breathing completely. The man in the leather coat stands across from my mom, one hand on the counter and the other waving in her face. I finally get a look at his face, and I don't think I'll ever forget it. His eyes are black but covered in a glaze like the dead fish at the grocery store. His nose is long and crooked, as if it were pointing to something on the ground. The sharpest chin I've ever seen follows in the same direction. A disgusting wart sits in the middle of his bushy black eyebrows. His voice is low but frightening.

"Give me the book… I will rip this place apart to get it," he growls through his teeth.

"Hey, leave my mom alone, freak!" I walk toward him fast with clenched fists. I have no clue what I'll do when I reach him, but I am not afraid. His cloudy fisheye gleams intensely into mine. His lip curls up in disgust at the interruption. He leaves without another word, the door slamming angrily behind him. The same calf-length leather coat blows in the wind outside the shop window. I've been staring my nightmare in the eyes for years, and this lanky old creep won't get the pleasure of scaring me. I say I'm not scared, but I'm trembling, and suddenly the ache in my head from earlier is back. My mom lets out an exhale and a cry at the same time.

"Oh baby, don't you do that. I can handle the crazies!" She runs from around the counter and wraps me in her arms.

"Mom, who was that guy?" I ask while still staring out the window.

"I don't know."

Who is this creep and why did he follow me? And, who the heck does he think is to talk to my mom like that? The weirdest thing is he looked at us like he wanted to hurt us. This obsidian is clearly not protecting me from anything. If it wasn't for my lemon-strawberry two-layer cake and these awesome boots, this would be the worst birthday ever.

My dad walks in with his and my mom's coffees in hand. "Holy cow, they are slammed at Witch's Brew." My dad looks at us and notices he walked in on something. "What did I miss?"

"Nothing honey, girl talk," my mom says awkwardly. She just lied to my dad, and now I know there is something to worry about. I take out my phone to text Nat, my fingers moving as fast as they can.

Me: *hello I need you!!*

Nat: *…ugh! My mom says I gotta help clean up.*

Me: *The creep I bumped into today was in here harassing my mom, then she totally lied to my dad about it!*

Nat: *What a weirdo! That guy, not your mom. Go to the police!*

Me: *I'm going to Miss Clara.*

Nat: *I want to come! I'll tell her to give me my money back, that necklace isn't working!*

Me: *I'll let you know what she says. If she's no help, maybe I will go to the police.*

Nat: *k. good luck.*

"I'm going to take a walk. All the sugar has me feeling jumpy." I raise my eyebrows and avoid eye contact with my mom. That was no girl talk, and that was no ordinary Halloween crazy customer. I don't know what to think right now and need to get out of here.

"Hey kiddo, be back before dark! There are too many people we don't know in our neighborhood right now!

You know the rule; streetlights." He points his finger to imaginary streetlights above us.

He got that right. There are definitely too many people in our neighborhood.

"Ok dad!" I rush out and let the door slam behind me with more rage than leather-jacket guy.

The tarot reader is only a few blocks down. The cheesiness of her storefront makes me second guess coming here. A neon crystal ball flickers in the window. I open the door and I'm hit in the face with the scent of incense. She has floral tapestry hanging from literally everywhere. It's so dark in here I'm surprised she can even see her cards.

"Hello?" No answer. What am I doing? I turn to leave but hear the faint sound of a woman talking from a distance. Miss Clara is walking a client out of her back room.

"Thank you so much." A young woman sniffles while wiping away tears.

"You are very welcome, love and light." The client leaves and Miss Clara stops when she sees me. The old woman wears a pair of small rectangular purple sunglasses. They match her black-and-lilac colored robe, which flows freely around her frail ancient body. Her white fluffy hair gives her a frazzled appearance that doesn't match her sudden robotic tone.

"Izzy, I'm so happy you came to see me. That crystal looks great on you."

"Yeah, well it doesn't work. You should give my friend her money back," I snap.

"Well, I think you know it isn't instant magic. You must believe in things for them to work."

I had a really hard day so far and I'm not in the mood to play her games.

"Oh my god! Will you stop? What is with you? Why did you tell my friend I'm a witch?" I get made fun of enough by kids my own age and don't need some crazy old lady spreading rumors about me.

"Well, aren't you?" she asks.

"What? Do I look like these people who dress up and come here looking for a witch selfie?"

Miss Clara sits in a floral print chair with her hands clutched tight around a purple cane and lets me yell at her.

"Do you just tell people whatever you think they want to hear to make money off them? Well, it won't work on me!"

"Izzy, why did you come here? And don't lie. I like to be frank with people and respect when people are just as honest with me." I don't say anything because I'm a little embarrassed. She continues. "Is it the nightmares you are having? Or should I say, nightmare?"

Her words stun me, is she psychic after all? "What do you know about my dreams?" My knees feel weak because the only people I've talked about my dream with were my mom and dad, like a million years ago, and Nat.

"I know that they terrify you." Her scratchy voice is uneven and makes it hard for me to understand her. She isn't wrong. She gets up from her ugly antique chair and starts to move towards me as she speaks. "I know you think someone is out to get you. I know that… there are secrets in your walls."

"W-what are you talking about?" I stammer my words.

Her hoarse voice gets louder as her face shows signs of annoyance. "When someone is trying to show you something Izzy, pay attention! You don't just look in the books, you look past them!" What the heck is that supposed to mean? She starts to hiss her words faster, spit flying each time her lips open. "I think you feel energy, Izzy. How do you feel in town square? Happy like everyone else? Or do you feel the wretched screams eating away at you? Do you feel the desperate souls reaching for you?"

Miss Clara is too close for comfort. She is so close that her glasses fall, revealing her gray cloudy eyes. I feel dizzy and something is telling me to run, so I do. My hands find the metal knob on the door, and I push forward with all my might, falling onto the rickety steps and stumbling down to the cobblestone.

It's starting to drizzle, and it hides my tears from all the happy tourists in the street. The sky crawls toward nightfall. A swirl of deep blue and orange mixes with the charcoal rainclouds, a dusk that belongs to the damp autumn. I walk back to Dark Alley Books like my dad asked. When I get home, I look in the window of the bookstore. It looks beautiful, even if there are plastic bats and cheap witch hats on display. My dad is at the register ringing in book after book for smiling customers. Kids are sitting on the floor playing with artificial crystal balls. Their faces bright with excitement, a feeling that seems so far away. I wish I could erase this day. I wish I could be like those kids playing innocently right there on that very floor. No Bony Witch, no one trying to hurt me or my mom, and no Miss Clara.

I walk up to the plaque next to our door and run my fingers over it. I feel the grooves of each word. Miss Clara was right. I do feel something. I feel it and I see it. I close my eyes and see a man and his wife. They are happily dancing around this very bookstore. When the woman in a beautiful black dress does a twirl, she winks at me as she makes eye contact. She is absolutely stunning as the ruffles of her floor-length dress sweep across the wood. Her black boots are visible with each kick of her leg. She looks just like my mom but also a lot like Bony Witch. If Bony Witch had eyes and actual lips, this is what she would look like. Warm and loving, but strong and fearless. For a split second, I'm not afraid of her. I release my hand from the plaque and snap out of my vision as the droplets of water dripping from the awning speckle onto my face.

Chapter 4

The sounds of laughter and too many voices greet me when I go inside. My mom is in the new-releases section talking to a bunch of college kids. I sneak past her, down towards the back of the store. I open the double doors that lead to our staircase and head straight for my room. I navigate through the dark by memory, my hand grazing the wall for minimal assistance. My room is freezing, and I realize my window has been open all day. This time of year in New England is tricky. The midday sun is hot, but the evening air is crisp. You need a sweater, but you don't feel like carrying it around all day. When the sun sets, the breeze blows in from the east, carrying the chill of the Atlantic Ocean through the streets. Just as you get ready to curse mother nature, you are hit in the face with the most intoxicating aroma. The salty air mixes with the scent of freshly baked cider donuts and lingering smoke from nearby bonfires. If Marblehead had its own candle, this is exactly what it would smell like. I close my window, hoping the chill will go away and the scent will stay.

My fluffy bed full of throw pillows and cat plushies never looked so comfortable. I don't think twice before collapsing face down onto the plush pile. The plants that hang over my bed appear wilted from the autumn air that stalked them all day.

"Oops," I say aloud to myself. I begged mom and dad for a real cat so they gave me these stupid plants to prove to them I could keep something alive. So far, I think I'm failing. The ivy's wilted yellow leaves and sagging vines are basically screaming for help. I dig around my duvet for my remote control for the fairy lights that decorate them. I put them on the dim setting and immediately think they look healthier, and I roll over onto my back. Twisting and twirling my new crystal necklace with my finger, I think about everything Miss Clara said. What did she mean by my walls have secrets? I suddenly think of the vision that played before my eyes when I touched the plaque outside. Was that real or another daydream? What's the difference? Is she really a witch? Am I? For some reason, I think if I want to know the truth, my mom's office is the place to start. She lied to my dad today. What else is she lying about?

Without giving it another thought, I slip off my boots and sneak down the hall to her office. It's only five o'clock and the shop stays open till eight, which gives me at least another two and a half hours. I open her door as slowly as I can because everything creaks in this old house and even though I'm the only one upstairs, I'm nervous. If my mom catches me snooping around her office, I'll probably be grounded, even if it is my birthday. I know exactly what she'd say. "Isabelle Luna Hoffman, what do you think you are doing? I know we taught you better than to be looking through my things!" I roll my eyes at the thought. So high and mighty, yet she lies right to our faces.

I walk over to her desk where she normally sits in the evenings with her chai tea. She typically sits in a green velvet chair, with her legs crossed, glasses on with her laptop out. Sometimes she has a few books spread about while she looks at them intently, scribbling notes in the margins. I run my fingers over the smooth dark oak, hoping to have a vision like I did earlier. Nothing. I try to open the drawer but of course it's locked. I plop down on the soft velvet and tap my fingers on my thighs, blowing out a long-exaggerated breath as my eyes scan the room. Then I see it, a door. You would never notice this door if you weren't looking for it. It has paneling on the bottom half, and flowered wallpaper above that, just like the rest of the room. The crystal doorknob blends in so well because there are dozens of stained-glass ornaments hanging about the tattered paper, which has been on the walls for at least fifty years. I'm getting in that room no matter what. I'll break the wall if I gotta! I don't have to do much because the door opens as soon as I lean into it. "She locks her desk but not the door to a secret room?" I whisper to myself.

I step carefully into the most beautiful room I've ever

seen in my life. Hundreds of white candles sit unlit on stone shelving. A circle is drawn on the floor in white paint. Floor cushions are set up against the wall and a collection of old-looking books sit on a small table next to that. How can I feel so full of adrenaline and so relaxed at the same time? Then again, this is how I feel in my crystal corner. I walk over to the books and pick up the first thing I see. It looks more like a scrapbook when I get a better look. The first page is a cut-out news article that reads,

"First of many New England women tried and hanged for Witchcraft. Alice Luna Young, wife to Joseph Young, hanged on Deadhorse Cliff. Mrs. Young's trial lasted for three days before her sentence to death by hanging. She did not beg nor cry as her neighbors did, because the devil was by her side. The town thanks our local constable Giles Whittenmore for the capture. Future hangings are scheduled to take place at Town Hall."

My mom told me a bit of our family history, but to read an original article just feels different. To see her name in print and my middle name attached to hers makes me feel more connected than ever.

The next page has an article that reads,

"Constable Giles Whittenmore receives large bounty for the capture of several women accused of dancing with the devil."

And another,

"Hysteria in New England as witches poison the water!"

Article after article saved, laminated, and put into this brown leather book. I pick up another book and see its contents without even opening to the first page. Picture after picture of beautiful women with long black hair just like mine. Just like my mom's. The cover has an enormous tree carved onto it, its branches curving and stretching to its corners. I open to the first page, and there she is. The young Bony Witch, with skin and full lips. She's even more breathtaking than she was in my vision. Her long locks look like a horse's mane draped down her back. Full dark brows preside over eyes like my tourmaline crystals. She has so much feeling in her eyes. I can hear my heart beating and feel the sweat dripping from my forehead. I feel her, I understand her. She was full of love, ambition, and courage. She was a healer, a wife, a mother, a neighbor, and a friend. She felt things like me and knew how to channel it. I'm not sure how I know, I just do. Under her portrait, the name Alice Luna Young is written in old cursive. I can only read it because I once spent a whole summer trying to learn cursive writing.

Each page is another portrait, showing the beauty and strength of the next generation. The very last page is a photo of my mom. She looks so different here. She looks carefree and happy. She's wearing a white cotton dress with her hair long and straight. It's weird to see my mom any way other than how I always have—her hair in a bun, lips painted black-cherry red and stuffy boring dress clothes that make her look like she works at the bank. I wish I had known the younger version of my mom, the one that looks like she dances in fields and laughs like Nat. Will there be a photo of me in this book? What will the next generations think when they see my photo? I think of my plain features. My almond-shaped eyes and dark wavy hair that I barely brush. I always wear black and now with this crystal, no wonder people think I'm a witch.

I look up and see a mirror. I'm not sure how it wasn't the first thing I saw when I came into this room. The full-length mirror stands in the corner, framed in thick golden brass. It has much more detail than I could have ever imagined, but the little naked angel babies at the top are holding their hands out to each other. I know for a fact, without a doubt, it's the mirror from my dream. It's like my body moves without my brain's permission and before I know it, I'm standing in front of it. My eyes meet the glass, expecting to see the dark silhouette waiting for me, but to my surprise, my actual reflection returns my gaze. I close my eyes and breathe a deep sigh of relief. When my lids open, Bony Witch is crawling fast towards me. Her dark endless hole of a mouth opens wide. She is crawling so fast from what looks like behind me that I'm not sure which way to run. The mirror begins to crack as she shrieks out. My knees are completely weak, and I fall to the floor. I crawl out of the room as fast as I can, my knees slamming the wood hard, slightly mimicking how she crawled in. The high-pitched sound gets louder, but I don't turn around to see how close she is. I just focus on what is ahead and as soon as I feel the wood of the door hit my forehead, my body jerks upright to stand. I slam the almost invisible door shut behind me. I am soaked in my sweat, just like I am every morning.

Chapter 5

When I get out of the bath, I see the blue glow from my phone illuminating my bedroom. Three missed calls and seven text messages. The calls were from my mom. I really should have checked in when I got home. I just couldn't look at my parents, and now I really don't want to look at them. My poor dad, just sitting there thinking he's running a regular bookshop. Then there's my mom, who probably just lies about everything and keeps a secret room with my nightmares locked inside. My nightmares, and my family. I've seen pictures of some relatives, but never like that. News articles with terrible stories, and what was up with the candles and circle painted on the floor? Does she just do nightly séances in there and not tell us? My hair is dripping wet and smells freshly of lavender and rosemary. The scent reminds me of being a kid and my mom singing to me while she washed my hair. What was the song? "Wash away your day, cleanse the bad and start anew…" I didn't think of it until now, but my mom was singing a spell. She always made our own soaps and sprays and said all these phrases while using them. "Izzy are you blind?" I whisper to myself. Mom has been doing crazy witch stuff forever, I just didn't notice!

I need Nat because I cannot deal with this alone. Then I think of the articles, and I think of town square. I think of Miss Clara and how weird she seems. I think of losing my best friend because she doesn't understand. I look down at my phone to read her text.

Nat: *Izzy, what happened at Miss Clara's?*

Nat: *Hello?*

Nat: *Why aren't you answering?*

Nat: *Omg, I'm freaking out!! We didn't make a plan!*

Nat: *Izzy!!!!!*

Nat: *Ok, I called the shop and your parents said you haven't come home yet.*

Nat: *If you don't call me by eight, I'm telling your parents you were at Miss Clara's and that you bumped into that guy, and I don't want to do that, so call me!!*

I really should have texted her earlier, then I would only have to tell her about the psychic's parlor and not the shop of wonders going on in my mom's office. I put on my softest, warmest, most comfortable cat pajamas, wrap my hair up in a towel, light a cinnamon-scented candle and call Nat.

The phone rings half a ring and Nat picks up immediately.

"Hello?" she answers anxiously.

"Hey, Nat, it's me."

"Oh, Thank God Izzy! I was so close to calling your parents. You know how scared I would have to be to do that?" She exhales noisily in relief.

Why would I even consider not telling Nat everything? She is like my sister. If I can't tell her, then who can I tell?

"I'm sorry I didn't text. Miss Clara was so creepy; I ran out of there so fast!"

"What? I need details, tell me everything. Did she try to make you join her coven?" she asks, leaving her scolding behind.

I stop to rub the lavender lotion over my calves and try to think about what the worst part of that trip was. Then I remember being sprayed by the old lady every time she said something, "What? No, but she was spitting while she was talking, and then she started saying that my walls have secrets and to look beyond books or something."

Nat laughs "Ew, I hope you washed your face. And a witch with secrets in her walls? She's nuts. You should have waited for me."

I stay quiet for a moment before reluctantly saying, "Nat, I think I'm a witch with secrets in my walls. I found a secret room."

She doesn't speak right away, and I know she thinks I'm just as looney as Miss Clara is.

"I'm coming over tomorrow. No way you're doing magic without me." We both laugh, and then I remember I still haven't checked in with my parents.

"Oh, I have to go, or else I'll be stuck in my room with no company allowed." My eyes roll at the thought of my mom and her many faces of disapproval.

"Ok, I'll be there before you open! Eek! G'nite!"

She hangs up before I can say goodnight back, and I toss my phone onto my bed. Now to face my parents and act like everything is fine, like my mom is not a liar and there are no secret séance rooms or dead ancestors haunting me. I've got this.

When I leave my room, I find my dad first. He's in the kitchen slicing up what is left of my birthday cake.

"There you are, kid. You look squeaky clean. You've been home for a while?"

"Yeah, Dad, before the streetlights, like you said."

"Good kid," he says with a wink. "The shop was slammed until the last minute. This strawberry cake is gonna hit great with tea, you want some?"

The thought of a fourth slice of cake makes my stomach turn, but I sit across from him at the counter anyway.

"Maybe just tea, thanks."

He's looking at me weirdly, like maybe he knows something is wrong. "Your mom said you were having girl talk earlier so I won't mention that you are acting strange, but if you need to talk, I'm here."

"Oh god, Dad, that is so embarrassing, why would you say that?"

He throws his hands up. "What? I know all about boys, heck I am one!" He never fails to make me laugh.

"Thanks, but no boys. I talked to a lot of old people today, though."

He shakes his head "uh-uh, I don't know anything about old people, sorry."

I want to tell my dad everything, but honestly, I don't think he could handle it. He's not built for this kind of stuff. He's sensitive and kind and the thought of his wife lying to him for the last 15 years might break his fragile heart. He won't be angry like me; I get that from my mom. Or maybe he knows, and it's just a secret from me, which also makes me mad.

"Whew, what a day!" My mom comes into the kitchen and kisses my dad on the cheek. She holds out her mug for my dad to pour her a cup of tea. Her nails are long and sharp, wrapped around a shiny mug shaped like a cauldron that says "Practical Magic". We sell those mugs in the shop, but she's never looked so witchy to me.

"Izzy, we may need your help tomorrow downstairs. The kids made a mess in the children's section today. They were so cute picking out their Halloween books and playing with all the gadgets… Izzy? You are daydreaming honey; did you hear anything I said?"

I peel my eyes off her red claws and look her in the eye. "Yeah, Mom. I heard you. Loud and clear. You need my help. Got it." I take my tea and turn to go upstairs.

"Good night, happy birthday Iz! Love you! And baby, don't forget to blow out your candles, I can smell them burning!" mom says with her brows pushed together.

I don't say anything and keep walking. She just acted like everything was fine like, "Oh, honey I need your help." I'm so mad I could scream. I don't. I hear my dad whisper to my mom "Here we go into the teen years, buckle up." Sure, blame me.

I shut my door and fall onto my bed. I can't possibly handle another thing today. But tomorrow, Nat and I will properly investigate the secret room. I blow out my candle and shut off my fairy lights to lie still in the darkness. I watch the gray smoke twirl a hypnotizing dance until it fades in the blackness.

Chapter 6

My room is still dark, but I can see the hall light is on, showing under the bedroom door. I don't even remember falling asleep last night because I was so exhausted. I sit up to drink my water and something grabs my face. Not exactly something, but *someone*. I've never felt anything so cold in my life, not even the Atlantic Ocean in January. Bony Witch is kneeling on my bed with my face grasped tight in her hands. The feeling of ice packs with razors on their tips presses hard against my warm cheeks. She holds tight to my jaw, forcing my entire body to remain motionless, shocked by fear. Her face is colorless, and this is the closest I've ever been to her black-hole eyes. I stare into them deeply because I don't have a choice. Hot tears run down my face, but I don't dare blink. She whispers fast and low, and I can barely make out what she is saying. A movie plays in her eyes of a twenty-something-year-old Joseph and Alice Young as they dance around the bookstore. Then the creepy man in the leather coat walks through door with an evil grin spread across his face. He takes off his hat and shakes my great-times-ten grandfather's hand. The men are smiling but Alice is not. Then I hear the whispers "stop him, stop him, stop him." I feel as if I'm choking and soon realize the angry black shadow is tearing at my necklace. She disappears and I cough so hard because I'm sure I've been holding my breath for at least five minutes.

I open my eyes and my room is bright. A different Bony Witch dream but a repeating vision. I swing my feet over the bed to get up and step in water. The glass I left on my bedside table is now on the floor with the water pooled up next to the bed. I touch my face where Bony Witch had her icy fingers in my dream. It is sore to the touch. I jump up over the water on the floor to look in the mirror and my face is just a little red on each side along my jaw. "Omg, that was not a dream." I stare at myself in disbelief. A pink scratch stretches across my collar bone, right around the string to my crystal. I put on a black and yellow striped turtleneck to hide the mark of the beast. To hide it from everyone else, but mostly myself. I throw my black cardigan over the turtleneck, hoping an extra layer will make me forget.

After breakfast, I rush downstairs. Nat is waving through the shop window. I open the door quickly. "Hurry, get in before someone sees you and thinks we're open."

Nat smells like her latte.

"Ok, ok geez. Don't be such a witch." She smiles big because she thinks she's funny.

"Ha ha, pumpkin breath," I snap back.

She waves her iced pumpkin "decaf" latte around and does a little dance.

"I brought you an iced chai, and your parents their regular because my mom said I had to."

My mom comes out from the back, "Good morning, Nat, I thought I smelled something delicious."

I roll my eyes and turn slightly away from her. "C'mon Nat, let's go."

"Not so fast Iz, you have a children's section to sort out."

I totally forgot I agreed to that last night.

Nat and I sit cross-legged on the purple carpet while we slowly separate toys from books.

"So, tell me about the room," she whispers a little too loudly for my liking while tossing a bat plushy into a bin.

"Shh," I hiss and stand to put some books on the shelf. I step backward and peek to see if my mom is close. She is back behind the register sipping her tea and writing something down. She looks deep in thought, so I talk freely.

"It's amazing!" I gush, "There were books, and family photos and candles, ugh! I can't wait to get back in there. Maybe Bony Witch will leave me alone if you're there."

Nat looks like she's going to be sick. "What? Creepy lady from the picture? Don't tell me she showed up again," she says with her eyes open wide.

I'm not going to tell her how she really showed up and even hurt my face a little because then I'd be on my own for sure. I run my fingers along the scratch that slightly burns under my shirt.

"Well, she showed up a few times, but she's technically like my great-times-ten grandmother and I'm almost positive she wants my help but has a really bad way of asking for it." Saying it out loud makes me realize that's exactly what she wants. And I know how to get her to ask me the right way. No more crawling up on me, no more screaming and no more grabbing my face! "Nat... we are going to hold a séance," I declare.

Nat smiles and claps her hands with delight.

Nat and I head over to the occult section to check out books on how to hold a proper séance. I pick the shelves and pull out a book called *Communicating with the Afterlife* and another called *Dreams*.

I start skimming through the first when Nat yells, "Ok boring, this will take forever. I'm just going to google it." Clearly, Nat did not grow up in a bookstore. I've already read pretty much every book we carry on dreams and their meaning, but thought I'd give it another shot. Her eyes go back and forth and her finger scrolls as she reads, "This website says, always ask the spirit to enter your circle by name."

I nod my head "easy, got it." I take out my notepad and pen to scribble down the next step.

"Izzy, why are you writing it down? We can just look at the article again," Nat says with her hand in the air.

I like writing things down in the best handwriting

possible. I have at least eight journals in my room full of lists and drawings. I put the pen down and motion for her to read the next step.

"Have your guests turn off their cell phones, tablets and cameras."

I give her the *I told you so* look and retrieve my pen from the floor.

"Lastly, thank your spirit for coming."

Exactly why I read books. "Seriously? That's it?" Looks like we are pretty much on our own. I shove the notepad and pen into my cardigan pocket.

Nat starts jumping up and down, "Eek! Secret room time?"

Usually, Nat's loud voice doesn't bother me, but this time I give her an aggressive "Shh!" Getting kicked out of the public library is one thing but I am not trying to get caught in my mom's office. We are right on schedule, because the shop has opened and customers are flooding in. "They should keep my mom busy for a while." My mom is at the register, so we are safe to sneak off without her noticing.

I open my mom's office door and close it gently behind us, as if she would be able to hear anything over the excited shoppers. Nat and I both gasp in surprise when we see the state of my mom's usually tidy space. Her desk is ripped apart, with its drawer open and papers spread about. Books are taken off shelves, the trash emptied onto the floor. Paintings of family members and parts of town are even taken off the wall. "My mom is going to flip!" I look over at the secret door. It is slightly open.

I walk straight over to it and hear Nat start to say "Izzy, No! Let's get out of—"

"Get the heck out of here!" I scream at the top of my lungs! The man with the leather jacket is standing in my family's secret room. He is touching our things, the things I just found out about but already hold close to my heart. "Take your filthy hands off my mom's stuff!" I demand. How did he even get up here? The shop was locked until I opened it to let Nat in. Did he walk right past us?

I try to take a step forward into the room, but an invisible wall stands in my way. With a wave of the man's hand the books and candles are sent crashing to the floor. I think he is trying to distract me but my eyes stare into his as I pound the invisible force field that keeps me from getting inside. A grin spreads across his pointy face as he snaps his fingers. With the snap, thick smoke fills the room and he vanishes before my eyes. Gone in a black cloud of smoke. The invisible wall collapses, and I fall onto my hands and knees halfway into the secret room. An article lies on the floor in front of me, with his portrait front and center. Giles Whittenmore, constable, and witch hunter.

Nat and I stare at one another in disbelief. A witch hunter from the sixteen hundreds?

"I wish I pulled my phone out for that! What just happened?" Nat asks, but doesn't expect a rational answer.

"He just disappeared right there, poof. Like a magic trick," I say just as stunned. "I wish you got it on camera too, because my mom is not going to believe this." She may not believe me, but I have no choice but to tell her. I am not going down for this mess he made in here. And maybe she could give us a reasonable explanation as to why this guy looks exactly like the man from the newspaper articles.

Chapter 7

I race downstairs to tell my mom, Nat trailing closely behind. Enough of this keeping secrets from me and my dad. "Mom! We need to talk, now!" I interrupt her and her customer's transaction. She gives me an evil look then smiles at the man in a vampire cape. He smiles back with his plastic teeth falling out.

"Honey, I'm a little busy here, we can talk later, ok?"

Will she cut the everything is great act?

"No, not ok! That creep was in here stealing!" I yell with my arms crossed. I think she knows if I'm willing to give this much attitude, I mean business.

My mom gives a nervous laugh and walks out from behind the register.

"Will you excuse me for a moment?" She turns her back to the vampire and scolds "Izzy Hoffman, what has gotten into you?" in a hushed voice.

Nat comes running up to the register with a smile. "I can ring these people in, I have plenty of practice." She gets right behind the counter and takes over my mom's job.

Mom pulls me to the back room, a little too roughly if you ask me.

"Ouch, will you stop and listen?" I say, pulling my arm from her grip. "I bumped into that guy in the street the other day and then he came in here yelling at you, now I seen him go up in smoke in the secret room and he trashed your office! Whew!"

"Izzy what are you talking about? There was someone in my office? And what do you mean he went up in smoke?" She asks, confused.

"Yes, up in smoke. Let's go find that Giles whittenwhatever guy and kick his butt. Aren't we witches? Don't you have powers?"

My mom looks like she wants to laugh but doesn't.

"Oh, sweety, did you get into our family tree books?" she asks. I can tell by her tone that she thinks I'm making it up. After staring at me like I'm a baby telling her about my pretend game, she continues. "Our great ancestor Alice Young was the first witch to be hung for witchcraft in America. We talked about this before. That doesn't make us witches. Now I believe there must have been a break-in, but smoke and witches honey?"

I would feel silly if I hadn't seen him disappear with my own eyes. I really wish Nat got a picture so she would stop looking at me like that.

"Mom—"

She puts her hand up to stop me, "Look, I love the idea of having witch blood. How could I not, growing up here?" She gestures towards the bookshelf that holds the tarot cards and witch books. "But powers? No, Sweetie. Just a love for positive manifestation, baking, and books. Just like the generations before us. Alice wasn't a witch either. It was all a terrible misunderstanding of women who thought outside the box back then."

So, she wants to play dumb. Ok. Cool. "How do you explain that man looking exactly like the portrait from the sixteen hundreds? Why did you keep that room a secret from me and dad?"

She doesn't even think before saying "My meditation room? Your dad knows all about my meditation room and our family history. Where else could I keep our family heirlooms? And I couldn't wait to show you one day. Just when you were a bit older so I wouldn't scare you into thinking we were some type of wannabe witches. Look at the psychic down the street." She opens her eyes wide as to say, *she seems a little out there.*

I open my eyes wide too because it seems *she* knows more than my mom.

"Izzy, give me a hug, I've got to go call your dad and the police. I didn't want your dad to worry about the customers getting out of hand, but wow, a break-in? I should have told him immediately. I'm so sorry you came face to face with a robber, that is terrifying. Thank you for being so brave and coming to tell me right away." She takes her hands off my shoulders and places one on my cheek. Her warm hand just reminds me of the icy one on my face last night and I can't help but to think of Bony Witch. Was she trying to warn me?

My mom is telling the truth. I know she is. Her truth anyway. The real truth is Giles Whittenpoo is looking for something that belongs to us, and he can't have it. Also, my mom doesn't believe we have magic, wrong again. I've been seeing Alice Young in my sleep for years and I know things and see things with a simple touch. That's why she came to me for help. I run back out front to Nat who looks relieved when my mom puts a "closed" sign on the door.

"Let's go, Nat!" She looks surprised to see that I am not in trouble. "My mom doesn't know anything. But I think Miss Clara does. I promised you a séance and we are holding a séance."

I leave my mom to deal with the police. I'm not sure how serious they will take my claim that "a four-hundred-year-old man trashed our secret room then vanished before my eyes."

I feel bad about assuming my mom was a liar, but she did lie about that guy coming in and yelling about tearing the place apart. Maybe she thought he was just a tourist crazy about our history? But then again, she also avoided my question about him.

Nat interrupts my thought. "You're so brave Izzy. I

can't believe you yelled at that guy to get out of there."

"Thanks Nat."

I don't think I'm brave, I think I'm sick of being scared. I hid under my blankets for years as an actual ghost haunted me. I'm over that. I want to do what's right. If that means helping this great-times-ten ghost of mine, so be it.

"Hi, girls, how's October treatin ya?" my neighbor Tim calls from across the street. He stands behind a wooden box that he has set up year-round. He runs a ghost hunting tour of our town in the evenings but stands outside to engage with the tourists during the day. Of course we see him, but no sign of his son Anthony. (Anthony who is my neighbor crush for life.)

"It's great, Mr. Hastings!" Nat yells and waves happily.

"Tours every night, let me know if you want to join!"

"Ok, thanks!" she says a bit lower.

"You mean, no thanks. He just takes people to the witch statue and goes on about the town's curse." I say, like Nat doesn't already know that.

"I never believed the curse of the witch statue."

"Neither have I," I admit. And now that I know for sure that my great times ten grandmother was the first witch here, I really don't buy it.

The curse of the witch statue is something a fifth grader made up, I'm sure. They say if you touch the statue without a smile, the witches will put a curse on you. Sounds like bologna they made up to get more visitors in town.

The kids in school use to claim I was the witch to do it, so obviously it's stupid. Boys at school started calling me a witch a few years ago, when I decided black was my favorite color and when they realized I lived in one of the oldest buildings in town.

When we get to Miss Clara's there is a line down the block. Nat jumps up and down to see if she can catch a glimpse of where the line begins.

"Hey, your mom likes staying busy, right?" I ask.

"Of course, this is her favorite time of year. Why?"

I take a deep breath and yell as loud as I can while still sounding like I'm just having conversation.

"Wow, did you say free coffee at Witches Brew until noon? Oh, what time did you say it was? Eleven thirty-five?" The family standing in front of us is trying not to look. I see them murmuring to each other and shaking their heads. I admit I do sound a bit robotic. "What? Free apple cider donuts too? You must be kidding, they have the best cider donuts in town!"

That did it for them. The dad has his phone out and is looking up Witches Brew on his map. It's only two blocks away so it isn't a surprise when they leave the line.

Nat laughs and shakes her head at me. Then she joins in "Yeah, and if you post a selfie out front you could win five hundred bucks!"

Within minutes, more than half of the line is gone. Nat and I cut in front of a few people who are not paying attention. I open the door to "Miss Clara's Psychic parlor" and lock it behind us.

"Hello? Miss Clara? It's Natalie Tavares and Isabelle Hoffman!" Nat calls out like we've just entered a haunted house in a horror movie.

I nudge Nat with my elbow and scrunch my face at her. "Why, Nat? Why?"

She whispers "What? I don't know, I'm just being polite."

I remind her that the psychic is going to be spitting on us as she talks so no need to go the extra mile.

Miss Clara doesn't come out of her back room, but she calls us in instead. "Come in, close the curtains and sit."

I can tell Nat is nervous because she starts rambling. "Wow, It's so cute back here with the little tablecloth and pillows. You could totally do YouTube videos in here. You know that crystal you sold me didn't really wo—"

"Silence!" Miss Clara hisses. "You came here to speak to someone, but it wasn't me. Do you want to get started Izzy, or are you going to let your friend carry on about my décor?"

I really want to like Miss Clara because I think she can help, but she is making it hard.

"Yes, I want to talk to Alice Young. What do you know about her?"

Miss Clara smiles a devious smile. "So, you took my advice. You went looking in your walls?" There is something about her gray eyes that make her look like she wants to suck my soul dry. I look away from her in case she can read my thoughts.

"I know Alice wants to tell me something, I just don't know what. I know that someone is after something of mine, again I just don't know what."

Miss Clara shakes her head letting out a sigh "I hope you can be more specific with this spirit, or we'll just be wasting our time. Be sure to ask her where the grim—item is."

Nat and I exchange a look. I know she is thinking what I'm thinking. I look down at my phone and see that Nat texted me even though she is only two feet away.

Nat: *Could she be any creepier? Let's do this thing and get out of here!*

I look up at Nat and nod my head yes.

"Ok, be specific. Got it. I'm ready."

The three of us sit around Miss Clara's round table. The lights are completely off, with the only light coming from her giant crystal ball centered on the table. She motions for us to hold hands as she begins to chant a sound that seems to be coming from deep in her throat.

"Hunnn, hunnn, hunnn." She calls in a raspy moan.

My eyes are closed, and my heart is racing. This is the first time I ever tried to see or hear from Bony Witch on purpose. My eight-year-old self would never believe this. I try to remember the vision I had of her and what must have been her husband dancing happily in the bookshop. I try to remember how harmless she looked. I tell myself "She is your family, and she won't hurt you. You can do this Izzy."

I keep my eyes closed as Miss Clara sways back and forth in rhythmic motions. Her chants are becoming louder and more song-like with each passing second. In a strong voice she calls out "We invite you, Alice Young, to join our table!" Her head moves in a circular motion, almost swinging around on top of her neck. The woman's arms stretch across the table and her wrinkled old hands squeeze ours almost too hard. Her shoulders move back and forth as she pulls our arms toward her and away again. It's like she is dancing in her seat to a beat only she can hear.

My eyes are closed but I can't help but peek out at her every few seconds to see how she is moving next. The lights begin to flicker, and I know something is happening. The woman's voice grows deeper and resembles an animal growl more than a little old lady voice. I can sense Bony Witch's shadow and I wonder if Miss Clara can too.

I open my eyes with hopes of seeing her sitting calmly at the table with us, maybe a translucent version of the beautiful woman from my vision.

Instead, a black shadowy figure is hanging from the ceiling above us. Bony Witch drops down onto the table with a heavy thud, sending the crystal ball crashing to floor. Shards of glass fly in every direction. The crystal hanging from my neck explodes simultaneously. The lights flicker from a twilight purple to completely black. With each flash of light, I see her shadow move in jerky motions, her long black hair swinging away from her as she moves. She's crouched down in front of Miss Clara, then darkness. With the next flash, Bony Witch is on top of Miss Clara, pulling the old woman's hair and shaking her ferociously. Nat never releases my hand, and at this point I don't know which one of us is shaking. Neither of us dare to make a single sound, even though no one would hear us if we did. The wind is howling, and Miss Clara is screaming words in a different language. Is she chanting a spell while being attacked? The next flash of light reveals Giles Whittenmore's face under Miss Clara's head of white, frizzy hair. Her eyes are filmed over just like his.

I don't care what the rules of a séance are, Nat and I are out of here. We leave the hurricane of a room behind us. Before turning out of the door, I get one last look at Bony Witch while she wrestles the elderly psychic to the floor. The dark shadow covers the fragile woman, whose feet thrash about from under the darkness.

Chapter 8

The arcade across town is small, dark, cheap, and full of local kids. The games are ancient and usually takes double the quarters to actually work, but they sell fried food and boba tea, so if it's a fair trade. We take a corner seat away from the games because the neon lights remind me way too much of what just happened. I dip a fry in ketchup and look up at Nat. She is not being her normal self. Her eyes stare blankly, and her mouth is shut. Nat's mouth is never closed. The first thing she does when we come here is snap a selfie in front of the Pac-Man game and post something like "catch me if you can!" on her Instagram. Then she wants to see who from school is here and who are they hanging with. I get why she isn't doing those things, though. When my Bony Witch dreams first started, I was terrified all the time. Sometimes I was too nervous to even eat dinner because I knew bedtime was coming. I don't blame her for being shaken up.

"Nat, thanks for being there for me today. I know this is super scary."

She looks around to make sure no one can hear, then inhales and exhales deeply as if she were doing yoga.

"I've never been more afraid in my life. In movies, ghosts don't hurt people. I never even considered the thought of her freaking out and hurting us," she admits, while looking down.

She has a point. Seeing a ghost is one thing, but watching it attack someone is a whole other level.

"She won't hurt us." I try to sound confident because I'm also trying to convince myself.

"Um, hello? Were we in the same room back there?" Nat asks.

"But did you see Miss Clara's face during that attack?"

Nat shivers. "No, I didn't see anything but a black shadow. I tried to keep my eyes closed but the sounds were just as scary."

I pop another fry in my mouth. "The sound was Miss Clara, the face was Giles. Creepy leather jacket guy."

She slams her hand on the table and yells "What?"

A table of cheerleaders look over at us then go back to sipping their pink boba drinks. I nod my head in a silent hello that they ignore.

"And check out my crystal." I hold up the necklace by the black string, carefully trying to show the broken crystal without slicing my fingers.

"What do you think happened?" Nat asks while finally joining in on the fries we ordered. "When the crystal ball shattered, so did my crystal. This crystal came from Miss Clara or Giles, whoever she is. I think it wasn't protecting me because it was doing something else."

"Omg, you think that creep was spying on you through the crystal?" Nat says, shocked.

"I do. I think Bony Wi- I mean Alice, was trying to get this thing off me for a reason. I think she broke it for a reason. And if Giles had the power to disappear, why wouldn't he be able to cloak himself as someone else, or even possess someone if he isn't human."

I take the crystal off as fast as I can and crumble it up in a ketchup covered napkin. Nat and I both stare in silence at the trash pile I just created on our table.

"Happy late birthday Isabelle." I look up to see Anthony Hastings standing two feet from our table and looking right at me.

"Thanks, Anthony," I say in a quiet voice.

"I commented on your B-day post, but you didn't reply."

I don't say anything because I have no clue what he is talking about and no clue why out of all the weekends in the history of long weekends, he chose this one to talk to me. We've lived across the street from each other our whole lives. We played in the street together as kids, but now that he's a foot taller and hangs out with the jerks, we don't really talk. Now that I'm dealing with a great-grandma ghost and a shape-shifting psychic, he wants to like my posts. (Well, actually Nat's posts.) I usually have a lot to say, but I choose to just stuff more fries in my mouth instead. What am I supposed to say "Sorry, being haunted by my great grandmother and stalked by the guy who had her killed.?" He looks at his friends and then back at Nat and me. When I go for another handful of fries, he realizes that I'm probably not going to reply now either.

"Ok, then, see you around Izzy."

He walks away and I hear one of his friends say "bro, I told you, she's a witch. Totally weird." The laughing that follows bothers me a little bit less than it did last year. Maybe because Anthony didn't laugh with them.

Nat burst out laughing too, but more with me than at me. "Izzy what was that? You aren't afraid of Bony Witch, but when it comes to Anthony Hastings, cat got your tongue?"

I exhale and cup my face with my hands. I can't help but laugh at myself too. Nat is right, when it comes to the paranormal, I seem to know what to say. When it comes to guys my age, I'm clueless.

"I'm not a witch!" I call out after the guys, even though they've moved on and are playing air hockey on the other side of the room. The cheerleaders give us another look, and I must have gotten on their last nerve because this time they pack up their drinks to go. "Or maybe I am, Nat, I don't know."

"Well, witch or not, you are definitely the coolest, bravest person I know. And you make the all-black thing look very chic." Nat smiles.

I take another look at the broken crystal that is now covered in ketchup. I think about Miss Clara or Giles watching me through it. How else would she have known about my nightmares? Or the secret room? And she did always seem to be waiting for me. How did Giles know about the secret room? Did they watch me go there? Did I discover it for him and lead him into the exact place he was searching for? When we were just about to summon Alice Young, she said "be sure to ask her where the grim—", then changed what she was saying. Whatever they are looking for is grim. I just don't know what that means, yet.

Chapter 9

I walk home from the arcade alone because Nat has plans with her mom for the afternoon. I wish my mom and I had plans for the afternoon, but things seem so awkward between us right now. I wish my mom knew the actual truth about what is happening, and it could be like old times. Just the two of us, down in the shop laughing and sorting books. Then it hits me: Why don't I show her the truth. After seeing Bony Witch for yourself, there is no denying it. If there is any piece of that girl in the cotton dress left in my mom, then she will want to help.

I crunch through the leaves as I stomp down the brick sidewalk. I almost walk past the witch statue, but something tells me to go have a look at her with new eyes. I wait my turn in the long line of people taking pictures. The couple in front of me is dressed in matching black jean jackets and the girl with black lipstick holds up her engagement ring in the photo. I feel like they are taking the longest, and after the twentieth selfie they finally stand back to check their photos. I step up to the statue. There she is, all ten feet of bronze. She sits on a giant broom with a smiling face and a mischievous looking cat on her lap. The microscopic plaque says, "In Memory of the young women who were tried for Witchcraft." It doesn't say anything about them being hung right here where this cartoonish statue stands. This doesn't represent the history at all. No wonder people can stand here and pose in costumes. There is no detail. This isn't a real memorial. It's just a stupid gimmick for tourists. Like one big joke.

I know the history because I read about it in our bookshop, or maybe I think I did. Miss Clara asked how I felt standing here in this spot, so I ask myself the same question. I close my eyes and take a deep breath. I tune out the guy behind me yelling at me to "get out of the way already!" I don't have a vision here and certainly don't feel a curse, but an overwhelming feeling of complete and utter sadness takes over me. I feel alone and afraid. My chest aches like nothing I've ever felt before. Where are these feelings coming from? I open my eyes to people taking pictures with the statue as if I'm not even standing here. They must have given up yelling for me to move. Again, I want my mom. I want her to bake me something and tell me everything is fine.

I leave the crowd behind and walk as fast as I can to the bookstore. The wind is really picking up now, blowing the leaves into beautiful orange and yellow cyclones down the street. The sound mimics the howls I heard during the so-called séance, and I feel goosebumps run across my arms. I can't get home fast enough.

After what seems like a three-hour walk home, I go straight upstairs into the kitchen, hoping to find something sweet. My mom is bent over taking something out of the oven. She has dozens of aprons for baking, but she is wearing her stress-baking apron, the one with pictures of little pies all over it. I look at the counter tops, and they are covered in treats. A tray of homemade pop tarts with pink icing, chocolate chip cookies (most likely the chewy kind), two different pies and a huge lasagna that she just put down.

"Hey, Mom." I say, probably sounding as tired as I feel.

"Izzy," my mom says with a sad expression. I walk over and wrap my arms around her flour-covered body. "You are old enough for the truth. And I'm ready to tell you what I know if you'll listen."

I don't remove my face from her neck, I just take in the familiar lavender scent of her skin.

I nod my head, rubbing my cold nose against her. "Me too," I say.

"I've been stress baking since the police left, so we have plenty to eat," she says gesturing towards the counter.

I plop onto the stool that sits at our high countertop. "Let me go first." I start from the beginning. "I've had bad dreams for as long as I can remember. A woman I called Bony Witch has been scaring me every night. On my birthday, she became more than just a dream."

My mother does not interrupt me, she instead pours me a cup of tea and slides me a perfectly pink pop tart. She has her listening ears on. I can tell. "I dreamed of the mirror in the secret—in your meditation room. She was always on the other side of the glass until now. She wants my help, and by she, I mean Alice Young."

My mom looks down and stirs her tea. "I dreamed of her when I was young," she confesses. "She terrified me. I did a ritual that I found in one of our old recipe books, and asked her to never come to me again. I was afraid she would hurt me. I met your dad a few years later and tried not to think of that part of life. When you said you were having nightmares when you were little, I hoped it was something else."

I look into my mom's eyes and see how hurt she feels. Then I tell her, "I see things, and feel things. Have you ever experienced that?"

"No," she says. "But whenever I made a recipe or performed a ritual out of any of these books, they've always worked." She waves her arm, gesturing toward the many recipe books lining the shelf about the stove. "What I said about us loving to bake is true, but there may be a little ancestral magic behind the recipes." The books are obviously old, and they resemble the books in the secret room.

"What is that one there in the middle?" I ask.

"Oh girl, that's my favorite. The end is signed by Alice

Young herself. The others belonged to other women in our lineage." She takes it down for us to look at. She runs her hand along the cover and says, "Alice was our great grandmother. The first woman to be hung for witchcraft in America. Seems unreal, to be killed for something so silly."

When my fingertips brush the brown leather, I know right away it is exactly what Giles Whittenmore wants.

Chapter 10

The pages are old and yellowed, but surprisingly not torn or frayed. Fancy cursive writing and drawings on each page give me a glimpse into who Alice Young was. I was right about what I felt in the secret room when I saw her photos. She was a healer. She healed this community with baked goods and small spells. She loved books and sugar, just like me and my mom. Recipes for "love stew" and "happy cakes" fill some of the pages, while others are filled with soaps for cleansing and renewal. You would never see this in a new cookbook or recipe blog, soup on one page and soap on another. It makes my mom and I both laugh.

"I never gave it any thought" my mom laughs. "I guess this is more of a grimoire than a cookbook!"

My laugh fades as I think of the word "grimoire." I think of Miss Clara and how her face resembled the witch hunters, as my ghost witch granny clawed her face.

"This is what Giles wants," I say, suddenly serious.

My mom looks confused. "Who?" she asks.

"The creepy guy, Mom. The one who broke in and

trashed your office."

"I don't understand, why would he come here now, looking for our cake recipes?"

I take one last bite of my pop tart and wash it down with a sip of my chai.

"Mom, do you want to help?" I ask hoping more than anything in the world she says yes.

She looks skeptical at first but takes another sip of her tea and nods her head in agreement.

We head into my mom's office after placing the grimoire back on the cookbook shelf where it belongs. It's been hiding in plain sight for years, so I feel like it's in its right place. The office has been cleaned up, the broken glass swept up from the hardwood floor, and all the trash taken outside.

"Is it ok if we use your meditation room?"

"What exactly are we doing Iz?" my mom asks with a worried look on her face.

I don't want to scare her, but she needs to see the truth, not just hear it from my mouth. I don't answer her. Instead, I kneel to pick up the portrait of Giles Whittenmore from the floor. I put the paper in her hands and begin to collect the papers that are still scattered about. From the mess, I guess my mom didn't have the police check her meditation room. A black circle of ash stains the floor where Giles stood, and the memory of his vanishing with a snap of a finger still puzzles me. I point to the black soot he left behind.

"This is where he was before he just… vanished," I say, recalling the memory.

My mom looks at the pile and then back at the picture in her hands. She studies the portrait and shakes her head.

"How? How could that man look so much like him? Why does he want our books?" she asks quietly.

Here is one I didn't see last time. An article from eighteen hundred. An article written by Annabella P. Young, the first female journalist of Marblehead, MA. She eventually moved to Portland, Maine for a bigger newspaper, or maybe to escape the witch history.

The Devil Walks Among Us. An article written by Annabella P. Young. Have you ever witnessed the devil in one's eyes? The milky texture their eyes take on? The grotesque sound of it willing its host to speak? I dare you not to interact with such beasts, but to write Miss Lavirne Telarousse. Address 616 Essex St, Marblehead, MA.

"Mom, isn't Miss Clara's Psychic Parlor on Essex street?"

She is looking through the articles but looks up to answer, "Mm hm, why?"

"I really think this is the same man, not someone who looks like him." I think of Miss Clara's filmy eyes again. "I think *the devil walks among us.*"

She takes the paper from my hands and reads the article out loud.

"That man's eyes scared me. I knew something wasn't right but didn't want to believe it."

"Do you believe it now?" I ask.

She nods her head yes while still staring at the article. "I'm sorry, Iz."

"Did you by any chance bake something with the word healing in the name earlier?"

She raises her eyebrows at me. "Girl, what did you do?" she asks, narrowing her eyes.

I giggle a little because my mom knows I can get into a bit of trouble at times, but this was not my fault. Not like when Nat and I dressed up like ghosts and hid in the cemetery, totally ruining Mr. Hastings' ghost tour. We were only nine, and I think it helped his business, if anything.

"Ok, so Nat and I went to Miss Clara's for a séance, but it didn't go according to plan, and I think Miss Clara was possessed by Giles Whittenmore."

My mom sighs deeply. "Oh Izzy, I need a cup of coffee and that grimoire for this. I feel like I am seventeen again."

Is it possible that I will pull that carefree spirit back out of my mom again, I wonder? She said that her spells always worked in the past, meaning at one point in her life she knew she was a witch. If she can be that girl again, I know we can help Bony Witch and Miss Clara. I may need to become a girl who admits they are a witch as well.

Chapter 11

Together my mom and I sit at the kitchen counter and look through the recipe books. We have at least eleven books spread about the wooden countertops. Some of them are open, with their covers resting on the pies and cookies that were baked earlier. My dad walks into the kitchen and gasps at the mess.

"Wow, I knew you two weren't fine after the break-in. This is the most you've baked in a long time!" My dad reaches into the cabinet for a mug and grabs a small plate while he is at it. I see him eyeing the cherry pie that isn't covered by our mess of books. "Why are all these books out? I don't think we have any more counter space for anything else."

I look at my mom, and she is peering out from the top of her glasses at my dad. "I'm stress baking, start eating."

No, I am not letting this go. She is not going to pretend that the break-in was a regular break-in and everything is fine. We are not lying about who we are, not to my dad. I take a deep breath and blurt the words out as fast as I can.

"Dad, I'm being haunted by super-great-grandma Alice Young and the guy who killed her is stalking us and broke in and possibly possessed the old psychic lady down the street. I don't know, but if he did, I want to help her and Mom does too." I exhale and fall onto the counter, burying my head into my elbow.

My mom thumbs through a page of the grimoire and without looking up says, "Like I said, stress baking."

My dad helps himself to a piece of the pie that he couldn't peel his eyes from and licks the cherry filling from his thumb. "I'm glad you two are spending time together. This month can get a little overwhelming sometimes and putting each other first is exactly what we should do."

I pop my head up in shock. Did he hear anything I just said? Maybe this was why mom didn't bother to discuss what really happened. Well, at least I tried. Maybe he thinks I'm finally letting the excitement of the town get to me.

"I told you Izzy, I baked and put all this behind me. He's blind to it, no matter what we say," my mom says in a serious tone.

Maybe it's better if my mom and I handle this while he watches the shop anyway. We sit in a quiet kitchen, flipping through pages and eating sweets like we have so many times before. It's almost like none of this is happening, only better. There are no secrets. I don't have to hide the fact that Bony Witch doesn't let me sleep, and I'm not on my own when it comes to helping her. Not that I couldn't take care of it on my own, but I don't like secrets. After looking through three different books, I find something, I think.

"Hey, Mom look at this."

She comes over and stands behind me with one hand on her hip.

"Rosemary Shortbread, hmm. I don't think I ever made these cookies."

I skim down to the bottom of the page. "To heal from within. When a passing spirit takes a piece of you with them, utter as you eat." The words are handwritten *"Redde animam meam quia pertinet ad me."* A chill runs over me.

"Sounds like Latin, most of them are. I can run down and grab a Latin dictionary," mom says, taking off her glasses.

Nat is rubbing off on me because that sounds like a complete waste of time. "It means, return my soul, for it belongs to me."

My mom looks up at me, shocked. "When did you learn Latin, honey?"

I hold up my phone and give it a little wave, "google translate."

Most of the ingredients are already out so we begin to throw them in the mixer. Butter, confectioner's sugar, flour, salt and fresh rosemary. My mom sends me to the windowsill to pick the rosemary fresh off our plant.

"Iz, we need this to cool for at least an hour before baking. I hope Miss Clara can hold off."

Nat and I left Miss Clara's hours ago. I wonder if she

is still being attacked by Alice, or even worse, what if the angry ghost killed her? It would kind of be my fault for leaving her there and going to eat fries like nothing happened. I suddenly feel super guilty for just running out of her shop. I pick two sprigs off the plant and begin breaking them into tiny pieces.

"Mom, do you think a spirit could kill someone?" I ask.

"I don't know."

I am not satisfied with her answer. Why doesn't she lie now when I need her to? I drop the rosemary into the mixer and try to breathe in the faint smell of it lingering on my fingertips. If we have to wait for the dough to harden, there is plenty of time to get Nat over here. I pull out my phone to text.

Izzy: *Nat! I told my parents about well, everything. We are going back to Miss Clara's.*

Nat: *Why?!*

Izzy: *Because I think she might be hurt.*

Nat: *?*

Izzy: *We found some articles and now I really think this Giles guy possessed her and that's why Bony Witch attacked.*

Nat: *What are you going to do when you get there?*

Izzy: *Feed her cookies.*

Nat: *???*

Izzy: *It's a long story. Basically my family can bake magic. Want to meet us there? We'll be there in two hours.*

Nat: *…*

Nat: *I'll be there.*

Chapter 12

Mom and I walk quickly through the crowded streets. The sea breeze creeps its way through the brick buildings and small houses that line our neighborhood. My mom pulls her sweater closed tight as we walk by the statue. We both shiver and I grip the tin of cookies tight under my arm. Nat stands three houses down from Miss Clara's shop with a coffee cup in hand.

"Nat, what are you doing here, honey?" Mom asks, confused.

I interrupt before Nat can explain. "Don't worry Mom, I told her everything. She was here for the séance."

Nat holds out the cup to my mom who gladly accepts. Nat looks down at the tin tucked under my arm and says, "wait, you're actually feeding her cookies?"

"They are rosemary cookies for healing your body after a spirit has passed through," I say with confidence. After an afternoon of looking through my ancestor's cookbooks, I suddenly feel I have expert knowledge in these things.

The closed sign still hangs in the window of the tarot

parlor, which isn't a good sign. Miss Clara could be dead, still possessed, or Bony Witch is over her corpse licking the blood off her long gangly hands. I don't like the sound of any of the possible scenarios I made up, and I'm expecting the worst as we push open the door. The parlor is dark and quiet. The only sound is coming from our footsteps and Nat's heavy breathing. I point at the backroom with my chin and my mom slowly leads the way. We are walking in a staggered line towards the back room like police officers on TV who are searching for a criminal. Waving our hands and using facial expressions to let each other know it's safe to make another step. But you can't fight spirits with guns or fists, so hopefully these rosemary shortbreads are enough.

When we turn the corner into the room where we last left Miss Clara, we find what we would have found if we were in fact a police squad. The room that is supposed to tell the future appears as if it has told someone's end. Glass from the crystal ball is shattered across the table and floor. The lights hang broken, and some have burst completely. There is an unwelcoming chill in the air that you can't quite put your finger on. Then I see them. Miss Clara's feet down under the table. Like the wicked witch after the house fell on her. Her purple old-lady high heels with the rounded toe point straight up. Nat and I gasp at the same time. She's dead, just like I thought. My mom rushes over to her side as Nat and I stay back close to the door. I've never seen a dead body, and I don't want to see one now, especially if I had something to do with it. Nat and I find each other's hands and grip so tight I'm sure our brown knuckles are white.

Mom bends down to check for a pulse and sighs with relief. "Whew, bring those cookies over!"

I finally breathe and put my hand to my chest. I have never been happier to be wrong. I bring the tin over to my mom and Miss Clara, who lies peacefully on the floor.

"She looks dead, Mom. This is creepy, are you sure she's alive?" I ask.

Nat, who was about to walk over, backtracks to the door.

"Yes, Izzy she has a pulse. Hand me a cookie please."

I open the tin and look at the words I wrote down on a piece of purple paper and taped to the cover. *"Redde animam meam quia pertinet ad me."* My mom picks up Miss Clara's head and holds her up in her arms, gently putting a cookie to her lips. She starts reciting the words in Latin, and I join in. Nat kneels on the floor next to us and joins in as well. We repeat the words *Redde animam meam quia pertinet ad me* over and over until Miss Clara starts to chew and swallow. Once the cookie is gone, we sit, and we wait.

"Oh, my word!" Miss Clara says in surprise. "What happened to my Parlor? Why am I on the floor? And what is going on?" Miss Clara sits up and looks around her once-sacred space. "My crystal ball!" Miss Clara cries.

"Miss Clara, let us explain," my mom says while handing her the rest of her now room-temperature tea. "Here, wash down the cookies, and we'll tell you everything."

Nat and I each get a side of Miss Clara and help her to her feet. I notice that her voice is soft, not at all raspy the way it was the last few times I came here. I look into her eyes, and they are kind and clear. The cloudy film is no longer there.

"Miss Clara, I came here a few times looking for your help. You gave my friend Nat a crystal to give to me, and we were here earlier today for a séance."

She looks totally confused as I speak. I don't think she knows what I'm talking about at all.

"I don't remember any of that. Did you do this to my parlor?" she asks.

"No," Nat and I blurt out at the same time.

"No, Miss Clara, we didn't. What do you know about Alice Young?" I ask her. The name alone sends visible shivers down her body. She seems so taken aback that it confirms that Miss Clara has not been herself.

Miss Clara looks at my mom and me, then at the mess of her room. "Let's make some fresh tea for this," she says.

Chapter 13

The four of us sit down at Miss Clara's now-cleaned-up table. We've brought in a lamp from the other room to have a dim light over us as we sip our hot tea. Miss Clara sits with a book in front of her as she begins. "Alice Young was the first of our kind to be hung for witchcraft." She has a sad look in her eye, as if she is speaking of an old friend. "They accused a good woman of terrible things. Dancing with demons, poisoning men for looking at her, tainting the town's water, sacrificing children, and drinking their blood."

"Did she?" Nat asks.

"Of course not!" Miss Clara says shaking her head. "She helped anyone who walked into her bookstore. She would hand out baked goods to the children who played outside and read them stories while they ate. The town loved her." She takes a sip of her chamomile and looks down for a moment. "Then a man with the darkest energy one has ever seen came to town and convinced the men that Alice was a heathen, something ungodly, a witch. It wasn't hard for him to convince them. A beautiful woman with books and charm was already a threat to simple men."

"How do you know all of this?" my mom asks suspiciously.

"I know because the story was written and passed down to each generation like a bedtime story. The women in my family have been reading cards and telling fortunes to the town's people for centuries. My sign out front may be tacky, but I'm the real deal. And our families have ties." She opens the book held in front of her and shows us a document signed by Alice Young and Ethel Telarousse.

A Bond of Sisters

A demon in disguise shall not taketh our blood. At which hour we hangeth, thou shall not rest. We shall not rest until that gent sleeps. For the love of our sisterhood, do not alloweth the folk of Marblehead to forget us.

Signed,

Alice Young Ethel Telarousse

My mom sits back in her chair and lets out a sigh. "I'm so sorry, Izzy. If I'd done something about this when I was younger, we wouldn't be dealing with it now. Alice came to me, and I buried my head in the sand. When I met your father, I put what was supposed to be a cloaking spell over him so he wouldn't dig too deep into our history. I just wanted it all to go away and be normal."

I can't help but laugh at the word normal. "Mom, I get wanting to be normal! But hiding the truth is not normal.

Having nightmares of your witch ancestor isn't normal. Feeding cookies to the town psychic after a demonic possession is not normal. We aren't normal."

Miss Clara laughs. "You are one tough cookie. You remind me of myself when I was a girl. I was worried that I'd die here in this town along with this oath. But you will help keep our word to our ancestors, Izzy, I know you will."

"Even though I don't have, like, witch blood, can I still help?" Nat looks around at us with a smile.

"Nat, you are helping. Who else am I going to squeeze when Bony Witch comes?"

"Oh honey, let's stop calling her that!" my mom says, shaking her head.

Miss Clara closes her book, and I can't help but ask her. "What does she want from me?"

The old psychic takes a deep breath and looks me in my eye. She repeats the last sentence of the oath she read us. "For the love of our sisterhood, do not alloweth the folk of Marblehead to forget us. This town turned into a mockery of our ancestors who died here, with no recognition of the wrongdoings of the men who hung them. Sure, I make money off the tourists. What else am I to do? But they should know the truth. I think more than just your father was cloaked. This whole town is cloaked."

We all nod our heads in agreement. Miss Clara is right. I think it's why I feel so upset with the statue and maybe even with our customers sometimes.

"Your ancestor's spirit has grown angry. I wouldn't contact her alone; it may not be safe."

I swallow hard at Miss Clara's advice and look over at Nat, whose eyes are as big as mine. I put my hand on my cheek and remember the night she grabbed my face so hard it left a red mark. She won't hurt me if I'm trying to help, I tell myself. Unless she has to, of course, like with Miss Clara.

"I think she attacked you because she was trying to help you," I blurt out.

Miss Clara reaches out to put her hand on mine. "Oh, I believe she was, too. She saw the witch hunter's spirit in my eyes, it was him she was attacking. The thing is any spirit strong enough to touch our physical world is dangerous. They've grown too powerful."

A truth I wasn't ready for. I take my hand from underneath the old woman's. Miss Clara perks up and adjusts herself in her seat.

"But you Hoffmans still got that Young blood flowing strong. I don't even feel like I've been possessed by one ghost and then beaten by another," Miss Clara says while taking a bite of another rosemary cookie.

Nat sends me a text.

Nat: *She sure looks like it.*

Izzy: *I feel so bad. Her scratches look deep.*

I look back up at the psychic's soft, pale skin. Her face is covered in markings left behind by the shadow of someone she speaks so highly of. I don't think her heavy foundation and dark pink blush can hide these marks.

"I'm fine, girls." Miss Clara answers our texts as if we sent them to her.

I put my phone away, a little embarrassed.

"We're glad." I say with my cheeks blushed.

"Thank you so much Miss Clara for the story and the tea. We'd better get going." My mom ushers us out of the psychic shop as she insists Miss Clara keeps the tin we brought our cookies in.

"Thank you, girls, for coming back for me."

Chapter 14

I take a deep breath and fall heavily onto my moon-phase-patterned sheets. I can't stop thinking about what the psychic said about Alice's spirit growing angry and powerful. The anger I could see, but if she is so powerful, why does she need my help? I look over at my crystals lined up on the windowsill. Even though I've been skeptical of their powers, I keep them in my window for the moon's light to recharge them. The black crystal that was used to look into my world lies wrapped in the ketchup-stained napkin and tucked into my nightstand drawer. I don't know why I am holding onto it, even though there is a chance it still holds a connection to the witch-hunting ghost. I don't want to give him any idea as to where Alice's grimoire is. I take the biggest book from my shelf and smash the remains of my birthday necklace. I sweep up the tiny shards and toss them in the waste basket.

Even though my body is exhausted, I pick a book from the stack piled high next to my bed. One good thing about mom loving books as much as me is she never made me turn out my light at night if I was reading. I could always finish one more chapter. Tonight, I am choosing the second book in this series about sparkly vampires to get my mind off ghosts and witches. The smell of its pages gives me such a safe and familiar feeling. It reminds me of cuddling up on a chair downstairs in the shop with my mom, her voice low and soothing as she read me stories from the Hans Christian Andersen fairytale books. We would light the fireplace and the crackling sound would sometimes become louder than the words she read, and I'd drift off into a peaceful sleep. That was before the nightmares started. When things were normal. There goes that word again. Normal.

A shadow creeps past my door out the corner of my eye. "Mom?" I try to say. My mouth is moving, but I don't hear the words. I don't even hear the creak of the floorboards like I usually do. I move effortlessly to the door and down the hallway in the direction of the shadow. At the end of the hallway, I see the black hair flip as she turns left towards the office. I don't feel like I am breathing, but clouds of white fog puff out in front of me in a rhythmic motion. The throbbing in my ears is throwing me off balance but I have to see where the shadow is going. The office door is open and so is the secret door. The glow of candlelight seeps out like sunshine through a meadow on a summer day. The circle painted on the floor is now lined with white candles waiting for me to sit. Bony Witch crouches down outside the circle with her hair hanging down over her face. Her black hole of a mouth opens wide to reveal a smile of sharp jagged teeth too big for her mouth.

A chill runs down my spine, but I don't dare move an inch. "What do you want? I want to help you! Just tell me how!" I know I said the words, but I didn't hear them. The smile leaves her face and she crawls closer to the circle, her claws scratching at the wood with each movement. She stares at me, moving her head slowly from left to right. The same as she has for many years in every dream she's appeared in.

I look at the mirror that stands in the corner of the room. In the mirror, I see the reflection of this room and the candle's glow. Young Alice sits where I sit. She holds a book against her chest with her arms wrapped tight around herself. She is screaming at someone or something in the corner of the room where I cannot see. A wooden bowl sits in front of her, full of blood. She begins to dip her fingers in the blood and writes a message in the circle she sits in. Her finger is trembling as the blood drips onto the wood. Her lips are moving as she chants, with pages flying in a circular motion. The pages from her book whip across the room and into the mirror itself. The candles blow out and she sits in the darkness.

I peel my face from my wet pillowcase. My neck and head are so sweaty that the little hairs that frame my face are curled from the moisture.

"Knock, knock." Dad pokes his head in. "Honey did you leave the hall window open last night?" I stare back at him confused, and he just shakes his head and closes the door. I must have been dreaming again.

Chapter 15

The last time I swore I was dreaming, my face was red from my nightmares grasp. I close my eyes and think hard about last night. I remember dreaming of the mirror, and before I know it, I'm in the hallway walking back to its golden frame. The smell of maple syrup and sausages wafts up the stairs and my stomach growls in protest of my direction. My body is telling me to head towards the delicious smell and the safety of my parents, but I continue on in the opposite direction.

The door to the secret room is closed. I extend my sweaty palm out to the crystal knob and give a slow push. The door opens, and a cool breeze greets me from the darkness. I walk up to the mirror and see the reflection of the dark room behind me. I look more tired than usual, with dark circles hanging beneath my eyes. My hair is puffed out inches from my head, giving me a bride of Frankenstein vibe. Then I see her, a shadow sitting in the circle slicing her hands with a knife. She makes a deep sharp cut down each palm, the blood pouring into a bowl that sits in front of her. She turns her head to look at me, her jagged smile appearing more sinister than usual. I feel my knees buckle under me and turn for the door. I turn around to get one more look before I close the secret door behind me and see Alice standing in the mirror with her arms resting on its sides. I want to help her, but I don't want anything to do with being pulled into that mirror.

"Mom!" I scream as I run down into the shop. I run so fast I almost knock over the entire new releases display.

"Slow down, Iz!" She puts her hand on the table to steady it from falling. "What's going on?" She looks over her shoulder at the customers who are browsing.

Out of breath, I say "The mirror, Alice, she cut her hands, there's blood."

She gets my dad to make eye contact with her then points to the register, directing him to take over. "Let's get some tea and see what we can make to calm down."

Mom puts a plate down in front of me with a small piece of a strawberry Danish. The smell of the chamomile has already made me feel a bit better. "I just don't know what she wants. I feel like she is trying to get me in the mirror."

My mom looks worried. "Izzy, I told you how she terrified me. It may be getting out of hand. We could always do the spell that got her off my case years ago."

I think about this option for a second. As much as it would be nice to get a full night's sleep without her shadow stalking me, I can't ignore this cry for help. What could be so bad that you haunt your own family? It can't be just the bond between Miss Clara's family and ours. Giles is after Alice's grimoire, and I want to know why before he possesses anyone else.

"No, I'm not giving up. It's time to end this cycle and lift the cloak off this dumb town," I decide.

Mom takes the grimoire off the shelf and opens it up on the countertop. "Let's look past the recipes and focus more on the notes and margins. There has got to be some sort of clue as to what we can do."

It's a good idea, but what about the clues Alice has already shown me? I think back to when I had a vision of Alice in the shop dancing happily. Then the time she showed me something similar, but Giles entered the shop. And last night, she showed me a spell through the mirror. This morning, a spell using blood. "Mom, do you see anything in there about using blood?"

She looks up at me through the tops of her glasses. "You did come bounding down to the shop huffing and puffing about blood. What were you trying to say exactly?"

I take a sip of my lukewarm chamomile as I replay the vision in my head. "Last night I dreamt of Bony Wit—I mean, Alice. She brought me to the secret room, where she showed me a memory through the mirror. At least I think it was a memory. She sat in the painted circle and chanted as papers flew around her and back to the mirror. I don't know what it means. Then this morning, I went to the mirror and had the vision of Alice sitting in the same spot, slicing her hand."

The tea is losing its calming effect as I tell the story. My heart starts pounding a bit harder as I recall her sharp teeth and demonic smile. "I feel like she wants to just pull me right in there with her." It could just be my imagination, but I swear I feel a cold tickle on the back of my neck.

"Honey," my mom says, "Let's go to Miss Clara's. We'll see what she thinks." She closes the grimoire and places it carefully in her "Women Run the World" tote bag.

After getting dressed in my usual mostly black outfit, the glimmer of the crystals on the windowsill catches my eye. The hematite crystal reflects the sunlight like a mirror. Its beauty is calling to me, so I pick it up and twirl it in the light. This crystal is supposed to be for grounding and courage. I think I could use some courage, so I put the smooth silver in my pocket. My mom's voice echoes through the staircase and up to my room.

"Girl, what are you doing up there? Let's head out before the tarot parlor gets a crowd!"

Right, today is Sunday and the streets usually get crowded around eleven am. All the tourists in their Halloween costumes start lining up outside the local restaurants, fighting for a space to eat Sunday brunch. I know Sunday mornings are too hectic at Witches Brew for Nat to come out, so I don't even bother to ask if she wants to come along.

We step out of the shop into the busy cobblestone streets of Marblehead. I love the feeling of the early-October sun. It's the perfect amount of warmth. You can almost smell it. But that may be the aroma coming from the drying leaves on the ground or the candy-apple vendor that has already set up shop at the intersection of Derby and Main. We cross the street towards the tarot parlor, and I hear my mom say "woops, excuse me." She has already shoulder-bumped two people on this walk. I turn my head and out the corner of my eye, I think I see Giles Whittenmore turning down Main St.

Chapter 16

Miss Clara's shop hasn't opened yet for the day, but the old woman is outside watering her burnt-orange mums. Without turning around, she says "Back so soon, Hoffmans?" Her manner is warm. I like her so much better than when she was possessed.

"Hey, Miss Clara, could you give a couple of Hoffmans an early reading?"

My mom nudges me with her elbow, and scolds, "Iz!"

Miss Clara chuckles and puts her watering can down on her steps. "I think we could make that happen. C'mon in."

It's a bit brighter in the parlor than it was the last few times I've been here. The smell of incense still hangs thick in the air but moon-shaped string lights and multiple lava lamps give the foyer a warm glow. Last time I followed my mom down this hallway towards the backroom, Miss Clara's almost lifeless body lay waiting for us on the floor. I'm relieved when we push past the beads to find the back room empty of dead bodies or ghosts. Hoping that there is something to the crystals and their healing properties, I stick my hand in my pocket to touch the hunk of hematite.

Miss Clara shuffles one of her many tarot decks and spreads them in a messy line in front of me. She pulls three cards from the pile, tucking the rest in her pocket. She flips the first card over to reveal a man standing with nine sticks.

"Ah, the nine of wands." The psychic sighs. "This card is perfect for you, Izzy. It means you are a force to be reckoned with. Ready for whatever comes your way."

I look at the man's face again. "Really? Because he looks sort of worried."

Miss Clara lets out a light laugh. "He is waiting. He knows something is coming. And so do you. We haven't seen the last of Giles Whittenmore."

The three of us nod our heads in agreement. She flips the next card to reveal a beautiful woman sitting between two columns, a strange looking hat on her head and a crescent moon by her feet. I think this card is good, but the hair on the back of my neck stands up.

"The High Priestess. This is interesting to pull right after the nine of wands."

I ignore the feeling of uneasiness building up in my stomach. "Why? What does it mean?"

Miss Clara looks back and forth at my mother and me. "It means, things aren't as they appear. You are ready to face the night, but it's uncertain what awaits in the darkness."

I almost laugh because that's how I felt every night, every time Alice's shadow peered back at me, pretending to be my reflection, every time she scratched her nails on the glass, and now when I follow her into the darkness.

"Miss Clara? Speaking of things not being what they seem. You mentioned how your family passed down stories of what a good person Alice was. How she used her magic for helping others and healing through foods. But do you know anything about her and blood magic?"

Miss Clara looks taken aback by the question, especially for a psychic.

Mom unfolds her arms that were resting on the table. "Izzy had a dream that Alice was cutting her hand and putting the blood in a bowl."

I'm beginning to lose track of which things are dreams and which are visions, as I call them.

"Maybe you could take a look at the grimoire to see if you catch anything we missed." Mom reaches around for her tote bag that hangs on the back of the vintage chair. "I know I put it in here" she says as she digs around in her bag.

I knew I saw that creep on our way here. "Giles," I gasp.

"Don't worry, girls. I have a feeling this is what the cards are telling us. Things aren't as they seem. Alice was smart. If that book is what this guy is after, she wouldn't have made it this easy for him to get it," Miss Clara says with a wise confidence.

My face is hot with rage. Who does this guy think he is? I thought the grimoire was a hiding-in-plain-sight genius way of keeping it from him. Now it's not what he wants and there is blood involved?

"I'm going to keep the shop closed today and look through some old boxes. There are hundreds of things passed down that I haven't looked at. Would you girls want to come back tonight?"

My mom nods her head yes. "It's a school night so it will have to be early."

The word school catches me completely off guard. How could I possibly go to school at a time like this? I give my mom the side eye that she usually gives me, and I'm sure my eyebrow is raised just like hers. The thought of waking up early after another night of following Alice's ghost around the house sounds awful. Maybe if we finally connect with her at a conscious level, she will let me sleep.

"Wait!" I blurt out before we are fully up from our chairs. "Do you think we could have a proper séance? Last time we tried, you were, you know, not yourself. And it would be nice to know what she's trying to say."

Miss Clara touches the scratches left behind from the last visit from Alice Young. Her gentle fingers brush across the raised burgundy trails on her arms. She rewraps her purple shawl and, surprisingly, agrees. "I think it's a must."

We leave the shop without ever knowing what the third card is.

Chapter 17

Me: *Hey! So much to tell you.*

Nat: *Tell me anything that isn't a coffee order.*

Me: *The Giles creep stole my family's oldest recipe book, Bony Witch showed me some weird blood ritual she did in our secret room, and we are going to Miss Clara's tonight for an actual séance.*

Nat: *whoa, whoa slow down. Are you ready to see that ghost again?*

Me: *Nat, I see her almost every day remember?*

Nat: *Yeah but like in your dreams or whatever. She isn't constantly attacking people… right?*

Me: *…*

Me *…*

Me: *do you want to come or what?*

Nat: *idk. I'll see if I can get out after dinner.*

I put my phone back in my pocket and look up at my dad. He looks so happy at the register, placing small stacks of books into our customized brown paper bags. He laughs and says, "almost forgot the free bookmark!" to almost every customer. My mom looks happy too, considering everything she knows now. She is helping a mom and her little boy pick out the best plushy to accompany his new ghost book.

I am at least five minutes into people-watching when a girl my age asks "Hey, do you work here?" I want to say "No, I live here," but I nod my head yes instead. "Can you help me with these crystals? Are they supposed to mean something? I heard they were good luck for my chakras or something."

What is she even talking about? I want to be nice because this shop is a part of me. I live here, but I guess I work here too. I am a part of this shop as much as Alice was. It is my store, and these are my crystals, but I suddenly feel a little excited to share them. Maybe it's the look on my parents' faces, like if they could choose to be anywhere in the world, they would choose this very shop.

I clear my throat and put my hand right over the bowl of hematite. "This crystal is for courage. Keep it in your pocket for a little boost, or sleep with it under your pillow the night before a big event."

She admires the bowl of tiny rock mirrors and picks up the biggest one.

"Cool," is all she says.

She adds it to her small basket filled with incense, a book called *Nature Witch* and heads up to the register. I blow out a huge breath and sit in the red armchair next to the crystals and tarot cards we have for sale. I've helped customers before, no big deal, but this feels different. Like I was happy to give a part of my giant collection away.

Maybe I have bigger problems now than trying to hold on to everything in this store. Or maybe this is what normal is.

The shop closes early today, so I head upstairs to take out something for dinner, like my mom asked. The sight of a blank space between the cookbooks on the high shelf sends a rush of anger through my veins. We should have left the book right where it was. What is that guy going to do with it, bake a pie? Then I remember what miss Clara said during the reading today. "Things aren't as they seem."

So, he thinks he needs the cookbook/grimoire but he's wrong? I pull down another book from the shelf. I search through Anna Thomas's book. Anna Thomas was grandma. She made some of the best soup you would ever taste. She passed away when I was ten, but I still remember her butternut squash soup and warm bread. I open its pages and think I can smell her for a moment. A musky vanilla scent with a touch of buttery bread. I search through to find the soup recipe and get right to work. I carefully chop the onion, celery, and butternut squash. Of course, this recipe calls for fresh sprigs of rosemary, because most of them do. The bottom of the page reads "Calefacies corpus meum, cor et animam. Habeo familiam meam et totus sum."

I google what it means, and I repeat the words in English as well. Going back and forth between the written words and "warm my body, heart, and soul. I have my family, I am whole." I recite the words as I stir the cream into the simmering vegetables. The smell is out of this world. I don't have time to make fresh bread so these frozen rolls will have to do. I hear footsteps on the stairs as I scramble to put the last glass on the high countertop where we share our meals.

"Mm mm, girl, what is that smell?" My mom comes into the kitchen with her eyes closed and her red-painted fingernails fanning the scent towards her face.

Dad walks in to add "Woo, smells like Grandma Anna in this kitchen!"

I officially made my first recipe out of these books completely on my own. Which means I completed my first spell on my own, I think. Maybe the crystal in my pocket gave me the courage to do this.

"Wow, Iz, this right here taste just like grandma's soup," my mom says in between a bite. A nice relaxing dinner with a hint of magic to help this séance along later. Maybe I am a witch after all.

Chapter 18

I can always count on Nat, because as terrifying as that last séance was, there she is on the corner waiting for us.

"Natalie, haven't you had enough scares this October?" My mom's words make Nat jump awake from her Instagram trance.

"Hey, if Izzy is there, I'm there."

My mom smiles at us and takes both of our hands as we head back into the tarot parlor. This time for a real séance. Not a dream, not a vision, a real meeting. My Grandma's soup and the crystal in my pocket make for a perfect recipe. I am ready to talk to Bony Witch. I mean Alice. Miss Clara has set the scene for a ghostly rendezvous straight from a movie. White candles adorn the tables, windowsills, and shelves. A new crystal ball sits on her table in place of the one that went crashing to the floor last time.

I feel underdressed for the occasion in my black jeans and cropped orange sweater when I see what Miss Clara is wearing. She looks the part in her long eggplant-purple satin dress. The robe she wears over it matches perfectly, with jewels running along her neck and wrists. The gems stitched onto her headwrap sparkle in the dim light. She reminds me of a painting you would see of a fortune teller from a long time ago. Even though the deep scratches are peeking out from under her make up, she looks beautiful. We sit in a circle in complete silence for what seems like hours.

Finally, Miss Clara says, "It's time, girls. Hold hands and close your eyes." She takes three long deep breaths then says slowly and confidently, "Alice Young, we invite you to speak to us tonight. Alice, we are here for you, and we want to help you. Guide us, Alice, into your thoughts. We invite you into our circle, Alice."

The stiff silence is sending a tingle down my arms. We all breathe heavily in and out in unison. I almost jump when miss Clara's voice calls out again.

"Alice Young, you are welcome to speak to us. Are you here, Alice?"

The silence remains, but a cold breeze passes the table. I know the familiar feeling and open my eyes. The lights are now off, and the candles have been blown out. Across the table sits Alice's shadow. My mother lets out a low shriek and Nat's hand is shaking in mine.

"It's alright, Alice. You are welcome here."

I hear the low fast whispers from the shadow that I heard on my sleepwalk. The crystal ball in front of us begins to illuminate the room. The crystal ball acts as a window to her memory, the same as her eyes did for me once. It shows us

Giles, breaking down the door and trashing someone's home, tossing away what little belongings that were there. A small child clings to their mother's side until Giles finds a book and rips the mother from the child's grasp. The child and its father run out into the road after them, screaming. A mob of people wait outside in what I think is our town square.

It must be a long time ago because the cobblestone is the same, but the roads are dirt and there are no cars. Their clothes look like costumes that people wear on a history tour. White button-down shirts and brown pants. The woman is in a white cotton dress. Giles holds the book up to the impatient men, and it ignites a wave of rage. They wrap a rope around the woman's neck as Giles tucks the book into his satchel and slips away as they hang the woman that he himself delivered to them. Dozens of similar images play, the times becoming more modern as they continue. Giles never changes his appearance. The last image shows Giles in a dark room with books spread about. Candles glow and the film is over his eyes. The table shakes violently while the lights flicker and the fast whispers get louder. In an instant, the crystal goes black, and the dim lights turn on. There is no sign of Alice Young.

"Thank you, Alice," Miss Clara manages to say.

The rest of us stare blankly at the crystal on the table. My mom doesn't move, and I think she is in complete shock.

"How's that for scares, Mrs. Hoffman?" Nat asks with her eyes wide.

Mom doesn't respond, she sits with her hand cupped over her mouth and tears in her eyes. "He took all their grimoires! He killed them all to take their books! Why?"

I realize now why I felt like he would hurt us. He would kill us to get what he wanted. He can't exactly hang us in town square nowadays. There will be no mob waiting for us outside if he claims we are witches. People already think I'm a witch, and all I get are snickers from classmates. People think Miss Clara is a witch and those same people pay her for it.

"Don't you see?" asks Miss Clara. "He is using the power from original witches to live forever. He's a witch hunter, but he's also a witch."

My mom removes her hand from her mouth and clears her throat. "We are the last original family. He needs our magic to keep going. Alice didn't want him to have it, and he isn't getting it."

The confidence in her voice excites me. "Let's get rid of this creep." Nat and I high five.

Miss Clara retrieves a milk crate filled with old papers from the buffet table in the room. "He must have taken the Telerousse Grimoire, because the oldest I could find was dated year 1700." She slams the heavy crate down on the table and pulls out a stack of papers from the top.

"I found these papers from the 1920s, they belonged to my mother." She places the small stack of papers down on the table for us to see. Notes from Miss Clara's mother on how to kill Giles Whittenmore. They are written in a nonsensical order, but clearly these notes were written for us now, over a hundred years later.

"A witch that feeds on its own kind… starve the beast from the magic it craves," I read aloud. What catches my eye the most is a drawing on the second page. A sketch of a mirror, a faceless child standing in front of it and a shadow on the inside. Anyone else would just assume it is the child's reflection, but I know better. The next illustration shows the child with their fists on the glass and the glass of the mirror cracked completely. I read the words on the next page.

"The calling for blood from the words within will seal the magic. The witch will feed no more." The words raise the hairs on my arms.

"Your mom saw me! She saw this. She knew this was going to happen!"

Miss Clara nods her head as she reads from a crumbled paper. "Every 125 years, this demon of a witch comes to collect the grimoires, soaking up what bit of magic he can to last him another 125 years."

Wait a minute, the first witch was hung right here in 1647. The next time he came around would be 1772, then 1897, then 2022. That's why when I turned twelve, Alice cracked the glass in my dream. She couldn't just sit around while this guy was after us. If she continued to haunt me the same every night, nothing would change. I have to break the glass, just like Alice did. "I know what I have to do," I say. Everyone looks up from the old paper like I interrupted their study session.

Miss Clara gives me a smirk. "Thatta girl."

Chapter 19

The first day back at school since the tourists start pouring in is always full of energy. The teachers are dressed in costumes already, and the school is decked out in jack-o-lanterns. Haystacks sit outside the entrance, and scarecrows perch on top of them. We are probably the only school in America to have witches for the mascot and live animatronics on our school lawn. The outdoor bulletin has dozens of flyers pinned to it announcing all the parties and events for the week. There is even an official town list of events, called "Ghoulish Gatherings." Nat walks up from behind and hands me an iced chai.

"Hey bestie, did you do anything after that séance last night? In the secret room or whatever?" She takes a sip of her pumpkin spiced decaf like this is a totally normal conversation to have before school.

"Shh." I hush her while sipping my tea.

"Oh please, everyone is totally wrapped up in the Halloween buzz, no one cares what we are talking about."

I look around and notice a crowd around the zombie

animatronic. A kid in ninth grade is pretending to be eaten by him while everyone takes pictures and laughs. Nat's right. Holding a séance right now would probably be considered cool, as opposed to weird.

"It's not the 1600s Izzy, you don't have to hide who you are. You should be proud." She stops in front of the haystacks on the way in and wraps her arm around the scarecrow to take a selfie.

In history class, Mr. Petri says, "we aren't using the books today."

The first day back in October, we always talk local history.

"The original homes built by captains are still standing. Some are even open for tours with claims of being haunted." A kid makes a ghost sound, and everyone laughs. "Then there is our favorite claim, the witches who were hung in town square. They put a curse on the town for all who touch the statue without a smile."

I don't even think before I interrupt. "The statue wasn't even there when the witches were hung, that's so made up. I'm so sick of this fake story. Why the heck are we going over this anyway? We aren't tourists."

He stops his story and looks at me in shock. "I'm sorry Isabelle, it's just a story. A myth. All in good fun. That's what this town is all about. What's gotten into you?"

Twenty pairs of eyes stare back at me, and my face grows hot. I replay the scene of the woman being taken from her home and dragged to the square. I think of how nameless and faceless those poor women are and how this town only mocks them.

"That isn't what Marblehead is at all. Alice Young was the first to be hung for witchcraft in this town, and dozens more were hung shortly after. Then dozens more missing every 125 years after that. You can look it up in the newspapers or probably online. Real women. Real moms, and sisters and friends. My house has been here since 1641, built by my great-great-great grandpa, Alice Young's husband. The statue was put up less than fifty years ago. Why would it be cursed? And if it were, it would probably be because their names aren't on it. These were real people, not some stupid joke."

Everyone turns their attention back to Mr. Petri awaiting a response. I look over at Nat who mouths, "Go girl."

Mr. Petri puts on his glasses and opens his laptop. He clicks away for a few minutes then says, "My god Isabelle. You are right. There are no names attached to the women, so we make a joke of it. I'm so sorry that you are connected to the history here and we are making a game of it."

Everyone begins to talk at the same time. Mumbles of how they knew I was a witch and stories their grandparents told them about my bookshop. I would have died if you told me this would happen a few weeks ago, but now I really don't care. Why does everyone get to dress up as a witch and buy witch books from the shop and celebrate the witchiness of the town without acknowledging the women who died here? We won't even get into the witch hunter. One thing at a time in public.

"That's really cool, Izzy," Anthony says from three seats over.

The bell rings after Mr. Petri tells us to research the year our town statue was put up and informs us that we'll be writing a letter to the mayor about getting names engraved on it. I guess telling a history buff the real history was a good idea.

Chapter 20

While most kids hit the Arcade after school, Nat and I saunter slowly to Dead Horse Beach. "That was awesome what you did in history class. You really stood up for all those women," Nat says while adjusting her backpack straps.

"I couldn't help it. All I could think of was what we saw in that crystal ball. They weren't bad at all. To tell people that they are cursing our town is wrong. I had to say something, even if everyone thinks I'm weird for it."

"I'm pretty sure Anthony said it was cool too." Nat giggles.

"Ok, he did." I giggle back.

I look up at the willow tree that almost hangs over the cliff. Its branches reach like arms towards the sea. I've sat under this tree so many times before with Nat and had picnics with my family. It has always been a special place to me, but today it almost calls my name. As Nat rambles on about how Anthony and I are so cute together, her words become a faint sound in the distance. I place my hand on the rough bark of the willow and feel a rush of emotion. My hair blows behind me, and I'm transported to the strongest vision I've had.

A crowd of mostly men stand around this very tree. Giles Whittenmore stands proudly, two other men with white hair by his side, a book tucked under his arm. A smile spreads across his face as Alice Young hangs from the tree. A child buries their pudgy face into their mother's cloak as cheers from the crowd die down. The top half of an orange moon rises over the Atlantic Ocean as the sun sets in the west. A black shadow that I recognize as my own reflection lurks behind the tree. The long silhouette of her hand rests on the bark like mine. Her haunting whispers echo in my ear.

"Break the glass and pour the blood. Seal the magic within the walls."

Her dark eyes hold my gaze until she runs toward me, and I remove my hand from the massive willow.

Nat's hand is on my shoulder as she yells for me to snap out of it.

"Izzy! Wake up, I think you are dreaming!" Nat's voice becomes clear, and I fall into her arms.

"The first witch wasn't hung in town square. She was hung right here. I need to get to the shop," I say while wiping the sweat beads from my forehead. How did I forget the article that said Alice was killed at Dead Horse Beach? Who would have thought she hung from the tree I sat under so many times? It isn't easy to run in platform boots, but I do the best I can with Nat trailing behind. We push through the crowds to get home, accidentally knocking a woman and her bags to the ground in our hurry.

"Sorry!" Nat apologizes for me.

We push through the heavy door to the shop and find a store so quiet, you could hear a page turn.

"Mom?" I call out. "Dad? Hello?" I say a little more urgently. "Something is wrong, my parents would never leave the shop empty."

"Where do you think they could be?" Nat asks.

I look around and have a terrible feeling in my stomach. It feels like I have a performance on stage in a few minutes that I don't know the lines to. I turn to Nat and place my hands on her shoulders. "Go get Miss Clara. But make sure her eyes are clear and not cloudy gray. Tell her something is wrong."

I peer around each bookshelf, expecting someone to jump out at me. The crystal corner is sparkling in the sunlight, bouncing the rays onto the purple carpet. I can't help but walk over and stuff a few in my pocket for extra courage. A whole handful of greens, oranges and blues stuffed into my jeans.

I walk slowly up the stairs with the familiar creaking of the steps creeping me out unnecessarily. Taking a long deep breath, I talk myself out of being afraid. "You totally got this Izzy. Alice is coming to you because you can do this. Whatever this is." The office door is open, and I call out nervously, "Mom?"

A muffled sound is coming from the secret room, so I charge for the door, my body weight hitting what looks like the wall and forcing the door to fly open. My mother and father lie inside the white circle, with their hands and feet tied. A piece of silver tape covers their mouths, and my mom motions her head to the left and tries to say something.

"Just in time, witch," Giles sneers. His filmy eyes are wide, and his features appear sharper and pointier than usual. His long yellow jagged nails wrap around a dagger. "You think you can trick me, little witch? I've been getting what I want for hundreds of years. The time has come for me to get the Young magic I need to keep me strong for another century."

"Well, I'm not a witch. And you don't look very strong to me. You look old and weak and you need to cut your nails," I snap while inching closer to the mirror.

Giles growls at my words, and before I take another step the room clouds with black smoke. These are the same thick clouds he once used in this room to disappear. His laughter echoes in the room as I start to cough uncontrollably.

"Izzy?" I hear as Miss Clara's hand guides me up from the ground.

"What happened?" Nat asks half yelling.

I was hoping I was dreaming, but the black stain on the floor and tightness in my lungs confirms I was not. "He has my parents!" I shriek while pacing the small space. "How could I let this happen?"

"You did not let anything happen Izzy. You are the key. You will get rid of the witch-hunting witch forever. And I'm going to help you." Miss Clara looks around the room angrily.

"We are going to help you!" Nat says.

Chapter 21

Dark Alley Books is closed for the evening, and maybe forever if I don't get my parents back from Giles.

The three of us sit in the occult section of the shop with a tray of lemon bars my mom baked earlier. The tray sits on an antique table that stands between two velvet pink chairs. I normally wouldn't be able to eat at a time like this, but the lemon bars are supposed to be eaten before a major event. I'd call fighting a witch hunting witch an epic one.

"Izzy, do you see anything in there on Giles?" Miss Clara asks, while adjusting her reading glasses and thumbing through her stack of papers.

"No," I say frustrated.

"I don't even know what I'm looking for to be honest," Nat admits.

I don't really know what I'm looking for either, but I don't say it out loud. I just nibble another crumb of lemon bar in hope of easing the sick feeling in my stomach. Miss Clara closes her eyes and puts a hand to her head. She stumbles, taking two steps forward and collapsing onto the plush chair.

"Miss Clara!" Nat and I shriek at the same time.

I drop my snack to the floor and move quickly to pick up her head. I pull on her soft paper-thin skin, tugging an eyelid open to make sure the eyes inside are still her own.

"Ew, Izzy, what are doing?" Nat asks, while filling up a cup of water to give Miss Clara. Thank goodness for the water bubbler we have in the center of the shop.

"I'm just making sure she isn't possessed again; I'm not trying to relive that day at her shop." Thinking of the ghost of Alice pouncing on Miss Clara to rid Giles of her body gives me a shiver. Miss Clara extends a trembling hand out for the glass of water.

"It's ok, girls. I'm ok. It's the cunning," she chokes the words out while her eyes open slowly.

"Is that what you call your visions?" I ask. I've only had visions upon touching things, or people, like when I bumped into Giles.

Miss Clara nods. "It's more of a feeling for me. My ancestors were seers, but I'm sure our power has lessened over time, since Giles took our oldest book and some of our power along with it. We were reduced to mostly seeing through the crystals or cards. My mother had visions— well, you saw the drawings."

The visions her mother had were very far in the future and probably looked like nonsense to others, because even Miss Clara herself hadn't understood them. She takes a long sip from the glass and looks over at the bookcase behind the dark wooden antique table. She stands slowly, using the arm of the chair for assistance. She gently glides her wrinkled fingers across the books.

"Girls, help move this table out of the way." She speaks in a far-off tone.

Nat and I exchange a *what is she talking about look*, but each grab an end of the heavy old table.

"Omg, this thing weighs like five hundred pounds at least," Nat says with her face turning red.

"Why do you need us to move this hunk of junk?" I ask.

Miss Clara runs her arms along the bookcase with her back facing us, her arms stretched up high over her head. She stops for a moment, glancing back at us. "Will you two help me? Feel around, this isn't an ordinary shelf."

I begin to toss the books off the shelf and onto the floor, an entire "green witch" section on herbs thrown onto the carpet. My mother would lose it if she saw this. My heart aches with the thought of my mom and my sweet dad. Giles had a dagger in his hand before they disappeared, and all I could think of is the spilling blood thing from the séance. What if I'm too late? My parents will be gone, and Giles will be around for another one hundred and twenty-five years. He'll be free to do whatever it is weird witch murdering warlocks do in their spare time. And I'll be an orphan, probably forced to close my family bookstore and move to Connecticut with my dad's family.

There is no secret button, no hidden doorknob or lever

to this shelf. The bookshelf simply slides to the left and into itself to reveal a small room.

The three of us gasp in awe.

"More secrets in my walls, just like you said, Miss Clara."

She looks at me confused, "I never said that."

"Oh right, that was Giles," I remember. I'm the first to step inside the dusty, dark room, my phone held up in front of me as a flashlight. I can't help but cough as I wave away floating dust particles.

"It smells like something died in here," Nat whispers.

"Mice mostly," Miss Clara whispers back. I cringe at the thought of little dead mice corpses lying about in the bones of my home.

"It doesn't look like my mom knew about this room," I say glumly.

With the white glow of our phone's flashlights, we can see that the walls in here are also bookshelves, like it was once part of the shop but was then closed off with more books, concealed from the world. Hiding books with more books. An occult section hidden behind what we call an occult section now. Alice would never understand *Yoga for Witches*, or *Tarot for Writers*. These books look older than all our cookbooks and grimoires that we have upstairs, older than the books in the I guess not-so-secret room in the office. These books have pictures of scary creatures on them, or symbols that I've never seen before. *Magicae Originale* is the first book I hold in my hands, and *Inventio Tenebrarum* is the second.

"Original Magic and Discovery of Darkness. This is dark magic stuff. Do you think my family was into this, Miss Clara?" I ask reluctantly.

"I think witches did what they had to do to protect themselves, dear." She puts her hand on my shoulder in reassurance.

Flipping through the pages doesn't seem so bad because it feels like we are making progress. So many interesting pictures of horned people and symbols that look like hieroglyphics. Pictures of space and stars with Latin words from cover to end.

"Um, guys? Is this what we are looking for?" Nat holds up the book to Miss Clara and me. The image takes up two whole pages. The sketch shows a figure in a long cloak holding their hands out as liquid pours down onto the floor around them. They are inside a circle, just like in our secret room. A protection circle, I've read. The words on the page are handwritten in English.

The words you seek are to be found within. The willow hangs low and will stop the devil's hunger forever. Luck be with you, my kin.

Alice.

I am visibly shaking as I read the words aloud. These words from Alice to me. These words that generations of women in my family did not find.

"Did I help? Is this something?" Nat asks excitedly.

"It's what's going to get my parents back and stop that creep forever, Nat!" I throw my arms around Nat and give her a squeeze while Miss Clara holds onto my hand behind her.

"I'm not getting any younger dear, let's get a move on it." Miss Clara suddenly says while letting go of my hand and ushering us out with the book in hand.

Chapter 22

I rush up to the golden mirror and can't help but feel as though I'm dreaming. I spent so many nights of my childhood both staring into this glass and running from it. Running away from my great ancestor. All this time, she was trying to tell me something. Why did she have to be so terrifying while doing it? Why couldn't she appear how she has in my visions? If she had, maybe I would not have listened. Maybe she tried that the first few centuries, but with no luck and Giles still stealing grimoires, something darker had to be done. Or maybe she turned dark because the situation turned evil by no choice of her own. A man pulled her from her home and had her hanged in front of the town for something he was in fact doing himself, practicing witchcraft.

She was just baking and helping the community, and here he was stealing family magic for his own benefit. No one should live forever, certainly not creeps like him. She must have had no choice but to turn to blood magic after she seen the threat in his cloudy eyes. I wonder what more my family could have been if he hadn't come to Marblehead at all. What would the other families have been? Would the town still be the center of the east coast's Halloween entertainment? Would we have skeletons and spiders hanging in our shops year-round? What if Alice was remembered for being the town baker and book lover that she was? Would there be a bench in town hall with her name on it for people to stop and read in remembrance of her?

I turn the glass knob to the secret room, holding my breath. The dark room spins as I put one foot in front of the other. My eyes shoot to the circle drawn on the floor, mostly because I can't face the mirror quite yet. The black stain on the floor pulls me back to current times. Giles has my parents and what he thinks is the grimoire to get the magic he needs to last another century. I hope he hasn't laid a finger on either of them, but the dagger in his hand tells me he had blood magic plans himself.

I look into the mirror, using every ounce of courage inside me. I think of the lemon cake that maybe Alice herself once baked before doing something scary. "You can do this, Isabelle Hoffman, because you are strong. You can do this because women before you faced worse," I recite these words confidently to myself. Manifesting, is what my mom would say.

"Go, best friend!" Nat yells from the doorway.

"Shh," Miss Clara hushes her.

A gentle breeze tickles the hair on the back of my neck

and Alice's shadow grows dark in the mirror. Her figure moves quickly as she runs toward me, but this time I don't run away. I take a deep breath and run the four steps towards her with my hands balled into fists. The glass of the mirror shatters to the stone floor. Some of the larger shards still stick to the bronze, but tiny pieces stick to the pink exposed flesh of my palms. Glittering pieces are covered in blood that drips down my arms. I scream out of anger, excitement, and pain. I've never felt this much adrenaline, not even when I finally became tall enough to ride the biggest roller coaster at the Halloween Carnival that we go to every year. The stinging turns to burning, and tears well up in my eyes. Through the blur, I see a yellow paper dappled with blood. A stained four-hundred-year-old secret message stuck behind the glass of this old mirror. Alice was literally calling out to me from behind the glass. The words are in the same handwriting as the words in the spell book.

"The words you seek are to be found within," I read aloud with happy tears. I almost laugh. "Guys! Look at this!" I shout excitedly.

"Izzy, you're bleeding," Nat says, examining the outer parts of my hands.

"Of course I'm bleeding, I need to spill blood while doing this spell to seal the magic." It makes so much sense to me now. I hope I am right, and this is all it takes to get my parents back and put an end to Giles.

"To the protection circle, Izzy!" Miss Clara yells. The warm light spills in from the office giving the white paint of the circle an almost glow.

Closing my eyes, I picture Alice squeezing the blood from her hands and chanting a spell, possibly this very spell written on the tattered paper. Even though it takes only seconds to translate, I don't bother pulling out my phone. Every second counts until my parents are home safe. I hope I say these words right, "Malos a capeiendo ligamus. Amor arcanum quod non tenes. Corda nostra Pulsant, in pulverem reverteris!"

Fingers interlock with mine on both sides and Miss Clara and Nat's voices echo softly next to mine. They both give a gentle squeeze and small drops of blood drip slowly to the stone floor. We repeat the words and our voices become louder, more confident as the broken glass from the mirror lifts from the ground and begins to float. The candles on the shelf light, and their flames sway and dance to the rhythm of our chanting. The paper begins to tear from the safety of its home in the mirror and blows gently around the room. The broken glass picks itself up from the floor and joins the swirling of loose objects outside of our circle. As quickly as these things happened, they come to a halt. The room falls silent behind our loud chanting, until the glass shards come crashing to the floor once again, startling us from our magical trance.

"What's happening? Did it work?" I release my grip

from Miss Clara and Nat's hands and step outside the circle. "Mom?" I call out peeking out into her office. "Mom!" I yell this time as I hurry into the kitchen. The bowls of left-over lemon bar mix sit out from this morning, the mix hardening onto the counter and whisk. Poppy seeds are still spilled out over the stove.

"Dad?" Panic is rising and it's clear in my desperate calls. Every nook of the shop downstairs is vacant. Occupied only by the books and props that grow dust over time. The excitement of the spell has worn off, and so has the kick of courage from the lemon bars. I'm left with an aching heart and burning cuts. The air stings the open wounds on my hands and arms. I fall to the floor in defeat, my back against the romance novels and my knees to my face. The black jeans hide my tears.

The sound of footsteps on the stairs causes a flutter in my stomach for a brief second, but that stops once my brain sends the signal that Miss Clara and Nat are here with me.

"It's ok, Izzy, we'll figure it out," Nat says with her hand on my back.

"We must be missing something Izzy. It's not the time to sulk dear, your parents need you. C'mon on now, up up," Miss Clara urges. She opens the book, putting on her glasses and flipping to the illustration of the figure with liquid pouring from their hands. She reads the message aloud *"The words you seek are to be found within. The willow hangs low and will stop the devil's hunger forever. Luck be with you, my kin. Alice."*

Nat screams and takes her phone from her pocket. She starts scrolling and I can't help but feel angry at her. I know she is obsessed with IG, but now is really not the time. Before I say anything, she holds up her screen to us. "Here it is!" she says, relieved. "I almost erased it because it gave me the creeps, but you know how hard it is to let go of pictures."

The picture she took of me on Dead Horse Cliff on my birthday. There I stand, awkwardly with a ghost looking down at me from the neighboring tree.

"Ick, it still freaks me out, but look, *the willow hangs low*."

"Ahh! Nat you are a genius!" I jump up throwing my arms around her for the second time today. "I totally forgot, Alice was killed at the cliff, not in town square like the women after her. How did I forget my vision? He must have taken my mother there to repeat history." What Giles doesn't know is, he's messing with three generations of magic, a super-smart best friend and a Telerousse witch.

Chapter 23

It's grown dark but you couldn't tell with the light of the supermoon illuminating the streets of Marblehead. Laughter and screams fill the air as we walk through the crowds in town square. My neighbor Tim is dressed in a tuxedo, cape and top hat as he guides a haunted walking tour through the small cemetery that remains in our small common. It is roped off, so the tourists all "ooh and ah" from the sidewalk. A group of women in ball gowns cross the street at the same time as us and rush happily into the local theater. Children run by in costumes, frantically shoving kettle corn into their mouths.

It's as though the night itself is alive with both a bubbly personality and haunting secrets at its core. Once we pass the corner after Miss Clara's shop, the noise settles, and the only sounds come from the wind in the trees and the crashing of the ocean. The orange and purple lights that adorn shop windows become sparse and the only light aside from the moon is the yellow glow from the streetlamps. Other towns have the new LED streetlights, but ours are the black old-fashioned posts from the early nineteen hundreds. Some would say it's charming, some would say it gives an ominous, abandoned-small-town feeling.

"Wait, I didn't grab the spell. What am I supposed to do when I get to the tree?" I ask Miss Clara, hoping she remembers the words.

"Don't worry dear, I took a page out of your friend's book and snapped a photograph, and a few of those lemon bars!" she says proudly.

"Impressive, why didn't I think of that?" Nat says.

"I couldn't do this without you. Either of you," I admit. "Thanks for having my back."

We walk in silence up the steep hill to Dead Horse Cliff. The sound of the tide moves in and out, rising from below as our soundtrack. I zoom into the terrible pictures Miss Clara took of the spell to try and memorize the words. Her phone is so outdated, I'm surprised it has a camera. As hard as it is to read, I'm grateful for this sort of blurry picture. Giving my eyes a break from the screen, I give the phone back to Miss Clara and close my eyes to adjust to the darkness. Glancing up at the willow tree, I see shadows in the night. There are two figures, hardly moving, but I can tell by the silhouette one of them is my mom.

"Mom!" I scream, out of breath almost immediately as I struggle to run up the last bit of the hill. Nat and I leave Miss Clara a little behind. Mom and dad are both tied at the wrists and ankles with twine. Leaves on the ground glisten in the moonlight with a wet, sticky substance. It is then I realize that mom's hands are cut deeply, and her blood still spills to the ground. Dad lies with his back to the willow, completely unconscious. I immediately rip the tape from their mouths. Mom sticks out her tongue and wipes drool with her shoulder. Dad lies unphased, even though the strong duct tape ripped out a few hairs from his upper lip.

"Mom, are you ok? Where is Giles?" I ask while squeezing her tight.

"I don't know, he's been rambling spells out of different books, including our grimoire. He's been gone for more than a few minutes," mom says with her eyes scanning the trees.

"He's growing weak. The spell in the grimoire isn't right. Alice brought him here so we can end this once and for all," Miss Clara huffs as she reaches and digs in her reusable shopping bag. She pulls out a container of salt and begins to make a circle around the willow tree. She shakes and empties the entire container as she ritualistically circles us, making a powdered protection barrier. "Here, everyone nibble a bite." she says, tossing a lemon bar at me.

"Miss Clara, look, there is Young blood all around the tree. He doesn't realize he started the spell for us!" I point to the burgundy stains that pool and splatter the tree's roots. I begin to untie the twine wrapped around my mom's wrist as Nat unties my dad.

Giles crawls on his arms from under a nearby bench. "You fools walked into my trap," he growls. As he crawls near, I see that his appearance has changed once again. I face a pale version of him that has ferocious yellow, jagged teeth dripping with saliva. His sunken face grows uglier with every inch that closes between us. His voice grows deeper as he snarls.

"Stupid, stupid girls. Generations of idiocy. So much power and you don't know how to use it."

Mom finds the strength to stand and hobbles to stand in front of Nat and me.

"I hung that wretched woman right here where you stand, and you too shall die here under the full moon." He approaches the circle, but his long gangly finger smokes as it touches the salt and then jerks back. Not that we needed any more proof that we were dealing with something non-human.

The black shadowy figure lowers herself down from the massive willow with the sinister smile that she's shown me so many times. Her teeth are just as jagged as Giles's. Her sharp claws scratch the bark on her way down. Her long hair reaches the ground before she does.

She bends her head slowly and takes a small step forward leaving one hand on the tree. With the other, she gestures with one finger for me to come closer.

"Oh, you've come to watch?" Giles lets out a hoarse cackle at the sight of Alice's ghost. "I will burn you all and watch them put out the fire tomorrow morning with all your blood coursing through my veins. I will walk as I have for centuries." He croaks the words as his opaque eyes roll to the back of his head. He begins a spell, and it is my cue to begin mine.

I walk hesitantly to the black shadow of Alice Young, who patiently waits for me. I put my hand out to her extended shadow. The cold blackness touches my bloody hand, which is still filled with remnants of shattered glass. A surge of power that I've never felt fills my body, and the clearest vision fills my eyes.

A blast of light and this very willow tree. A spring day and my mom and I lie beneath it with a blanket and a pile of books. She gets up and takes my hand, where we dance around the tree in white cotton dresses. Her teeth are bright against her dark lipstick as she laughs. She stops to tuck a daisy behind my ear. The sun grows warm against my skin, and I look down at my tanned bare feet in the grass. My heart flutters with the love that I'm consumed by. We stop to put the rest of the daisies against a stone sticking out from the ground next to the tree. The stone reads, "In Loving Memory of Alice Young 1647, Leanne Black 1647, Ethel Telarousse 1647, Agnus Telarousse 1772, Lydia and Portia Cromwell 1897. If not for these souls, the town of Marblehead would not be."

I open my eyes to see that the warmth of the sun is in fact heat from the fire that Giles has started around our protection circle. Screams fill the air as my mom, Miss Clara and Nat all try to snap me out of my vision.

"Everyone put your hands on the tree!" I struggle to

scream against the wind that whips my hair into my mouth.

The hands of the old psychic collapse onto the rugged bark. "Now, Izzy!" she yells, prompting me to start the spell.

Nat and my mom place their palms on the tree, my mom adding more of our blood onto the sacred willow, feeding it the power to seal our magic. Alice's black silhouette stands next to me with her ghostly fingers holding tight to the tree as well. She gives me a nod of approval.

I close my eyes tight and whisper the words, "Malos a capeiendo ligamus. Amor arcanum quod non tenes. Corda nostra Pulsant, in pulverem reverteris!"

I hear the whispers from the black shadow as she joins in to stop Giles from hurting any other witch. The five of us whisper a demonic-sounding spell while flames grow rapidly around us. Our whispers grow to screams as our desire to end this intensifies. The power of love, family and magic is far superior to that of a decrepit warlock ghost. My dad lies under the tree, totally oblivious, as if it were just a regular night camping out in the woods. He doesn't stir a bit as the wind howls, the flames dance angrily, and we shout. We shout and chant like our lives depend on it, until our throats grow dry and our voices crack.

"I bind the evil from taking what is ours! Love is the secret that you do not hold! As our hearts beat, to dust you shall return!"

The groans from the devil himself seem to grow quieter as the fire dies down. We don't stop chanting until the last bit of smoke clears and Alice lets go of the tree. She looks down at me with her black-hole eyes, and I know she is proud. For a moment she appears as she did from an earlier vision. A beautiful woman with full lips and long black hair. She reaches out to touch my hand one last time. I stare back into her dark eyes, and I'm grateful to see her this way. A weight lifts from the thick air and she is gone. It rains ash like confetti after the Halloween parade in town.

Miss Clara falls to the ground, and my mom bends down immediately to help. "Miss Clara! Are you ok?"

"I'm seventy-three years old, I can't stand for another minute," she says, relieved.

My mom and I both sigh with similar relief.

The moon shines with an orange glow, almost like it stole the hue from the fire and took it for us to hold onto. The only sign of Giles Whittenmore is a bit of soot where he once was. Dust is all that is left of the man who stole the lives of so many. He died here, starving for the magic that he had sucked from us for centuries. His final moments were at the foot of the very tree where he killed the first witch of Marblehead. This place will be special to our family and this town for forever.

"How do we know he's gone for real?" Nat asks suspiciously.

"He's gone," I say, "and so is Alice." I look up at the willow that suddenly feels like a part of me. I don't think I will see her lurking in my sleep the way I have for so long.

"What are we doing here?" my dad says, opening his eyes and sitting up against the tree. "I was having the weirdest dream," he says and trails off, confused.

"Oh, just fighting an evil witch hunter and starving him of our ancestral magic, preventing him from living for another 125 years," I mumble.

"Oh. I think I'm still dreaming. That's ok," my dad says while slowly standing. He stretches his arms up over his head and his back cracks in several places, causing him to hunch and lean on the tree. "Yow, ok, not sleeping."

We laugh a real laugh, straight from our stomachs. Nat puts her arms around me and snaps a selfie.

"Don't worry, this is just for us. The night we saved all the future witches from the ugliest man I've ever seen."

The photo is perfect. The flash picks up the orange glow instead of drowning it out, giving us a natural filter. I know Nat will never share this one, because you can see everyone in the background. A totally perfect photo bomb from the most important people in my life. My mom holding my dad's hands with a look in her eye like a schoolgirl staring at her first crush. My dad looking at Miss Clara, totally confused as to why we are at Dead Horse Cliff with the town tarot reader. Miss Clara leaning against the tree, looking like a ghost herself, in her beautiful green flowy skirt, crystals hanging from her neck.

I stare a bit longer, looking for Bony Witch. The ghost of Alice Young. There is no sign of her dark shadow hanging above in the branches. There is nothing lurking from behind, no long fingers stretched out casting shadows on the trees. There is nothing left of her, except for what I feel inside. Her spirit can rest, and each night so will I.

Chapter 24

One year later...

I know my mom said she'd tone it down a bit the next birthday, but I had a feeling I couldn't trust that. "Not only did my parents completely almost rip the door off its hinges this morning in the most ridiculous of happy birthdays I've ever seen, but they brought the pancakes up to my room!" I vent to Nat and Anthony on our walk home from school.

"Omg! Did your dad do the cape thing?" Nat asks while sipping her pumpkin spice latte.

"You know he did!" I laugh.

"Cape thing? What goes on in that bookstore of yours?" Anthony pipes in.

"Everything you think would go on in an old witchy bookshop," I wink.

I say my goodbyes at the same place we've been parting ways on our walks home, at the witch statue in town square. It's October first, so naturally dozens of tourists are in our way, taking a million pictures.

I kick the few leaves that are resting on the ground just to hear them move. There is hardly a crunch to them yet, but they do have the nutty smell I crave. I take a deep breath and inhale the pure magic of this day. I know my lemon strawberry cake is waiting for me at home and I can't wait for a slice, or four.

When I get home, there is a line outside Dark Alley Books, stretching all the way around the corner. Everyone wants to visit the shop belonging to the first witch to be hung for witchcraft on the east coast. They mostly want to come in and take a picture in front of our "secret occult section," which is blocked off with a red velvet rope. People who identify as witches today come and say they feel a connection to the place. They load up a basket with herbs, crystals, and books. Since I am the crystal expert, I'm there on the weekends offering advice on which stone is best for each intention. Who knows, maybe Miss Clara will teach me to read tarot cards since we share the cunning gift.

A girl of maybe sixteen reads the print under the portrait of Alice Young that hangs on the wall in our occult section and just outside the original occult room. We haven't touched much out of respect for our ancestors, but we go in to turn on the artificial candles that flicker to give just enough light.

"We were taught to fear the witches instead of the men who hanged them… that's so sad," she says with a genuine look in her eyes.

"It is sad. But it's important to know the truth." The truth is, I'm glad I come from a long line of witches. I'm glad that when tourists come to Dark Alley Books, they see portraits of the women who started it all. They are almost forced to look into the haunting eyes of each portrait before buying their witch souvenirs. "That's my great-times-ten grandmother," I state proudly. "She owned this bookshop and even sold baked treats out of it." I hand the girl an individually wrapped chocolate chip cookie that I baked myself last night.

"Thanks. She was beautiful." She looks back at the portrait in admiration.

"Thanks," I say too.

"Izzy, let's go, honey!" Mom calls from the door.

We have a new tradition for my birthday. No matter how busy the shop is, we are going to go to the willow tree to have a picnic. Mom said just the two of us, to celebrate Alice and all the women after her. We will go and lay flowers at the stone that now sits on the cliff. We will recite the names aloud that are carefully engraved, thanks to the letters my class wrote to the mayor. Instead of having the names listed on a fictional witch in town square, everyone agreed these women deserved their own memorial. We will feast on foods that heal from the inside out, straight from our cookbooks. We'll read spells out of the same books. We'll dance happily if we feel like it.

As fun as the thought of reliving the vision I had of my

mom and I dancing carelessly around the willow is, I don't think it would feel right.

"Izzy, what's going on?" Mom asks as we approach the top of the hill.

Miss Clara and Nat sit out on a blanket waiting for us, and wave as soon as our faces pop over the hill.

"If having a picnic on your birthday with your mom, bestie and the town psychic isn't normal, then I don't want normal." I cross my arms in artificial protest.

"Oh, I agree." Mom flips her flowing hair and the faint scent of lavender wafts in the air. While the tourists below celebrate the witchiness of Marblehead, so will the descendants of the original witches.

www.ingramcontent.com/pod-product-compliance
Lightning Source LLC
Chambersburg PA
CBHW061452210726
48287CB00007B/2480

9 781953 971852